D0276877

THE
IMPORTANCE
OF
BEING
EARNEST

By the same author:

THE GENTLE PLANET (*poems*)

PLATONOV (*play: adapted from Chekhov*)

AUSTRALIAN STORIES OF TODAY (*ed.*)

OPERA 66 (*ed.*)

PLAYING MY PART BY FRIDA LEIDER (*trans.*)

FIFTY WORKS OF ENGLISH LITERATURE WE COULD DO WITHOUT
(*with Brigid Brophy and Michael Levey*)

KAFKA

SWANSONG (*poems: illustrated by Sidney Nolan*)

THE COMPLETE OPERAS OF VERDI

NED KELLY

AUSTRALIA, NEW ZEALAND AND THE SOUTH PACIFIC (*ed.*)

LETTERS OF GIUSEPPE VERDI (*trans. and ed.*)

THE BRAM STOKER BEDSIDE COMPANION (*ed.*)

STORIES AND ESSAYS BY RICHARD WAGNER (*trans. and ed.*)

THE CONCERT SONG COMPANION

MASTERPIECES OF NOLAN

MASTERPIECES OF DRYSDALE

MASTERPIECES OF DOBELL

WAGNER AND HIS WORLD

VERDI

DICTIONARY OF COMPOSERS (*ed.*)

THE COMPLETE OPERAS OF MOZART

RIGOLETTO ('*Masterworks of Opera*' series)

THE OPERA HOUSE ALBUM

W. H. AUDEN: THE LIFE OF A POET

KLEMPERER STORIES (*with Kenneth Thomson*)

THE COMPLETE OPERAS OF PUCCINI

THE LIFE AND CRIMES OF AGATHA CHRISTIE

THE ROUND DANCE AND OTHER PLAYS BY ARTHUR SCHNITZLER (*trans.*)

THE WORLD THEATRE OF WAGNER

HOW TO ENJOY OPERA

THE DICTIONARY OF OPERA

LETTER TO W. H. AUDEN AND OTHER POEMS

SCHUBERT AND HIS VIENNA

VERDI: A LIFE IN THE THEATRE

GIVING IT AWAY (*memoirs*)

THE COMPLETE OPERAS OF STRAUSS

THE COMPLETE OPERAS OF WAGNER

THE BEL CANTO OPERAS

THE PINK DANUBE (*novel*)

BLACK COFFEE (*novel: adapted from Agatha Christie*)

THE UNEXPECTED GUEST (*novel: adapted from Agatha Christie*)

THE
IMPORTANCE
OF
BEING
EARNEST

A trivial novel for serious people
by

CHARLES OSBORNE

adapted from the play by

with an introduction by

BARRY HUMPHRIES

MICHAEL O'MARA BOOKS LIMITED

For
KEN THOMSON
who hopes this exercise
will have stopped me
from continually quoting
from the play

First published in Great Britain in 1999 by
Michael O'Mara Books Limited
9 Lion Yard
Tremadoc Road
London SW4 7NQ

A CIP catalogue record for this book is available
from the British Library

ISBN 1-85479-476-0

1 3 5 7 9 10 8 6 4 2

Typeset by The Florence Group, Stoodleigh, Devon
Printed and bound by WSOY, Finland

THE PERSONS
OF THE STORY

JOHN WORTHING, J.P.   LADY BRACKNELL

ALGERNON MONCRIEFF   HON. GWENDOLEN FAIRFAX

REV. CANON CHASUBLE, D.D.   CECILY CARDEW

MERRIMAN, butler   MISS PRISM, governess

LANE, manservant

A BABY IN A HAMPER.

On Monday a man took a hamper to the goods department of the Great Northern Railway, Kings Cross, and requested that it should be forwarded to a lady at Richmond. A short time afterwards one of the officials put the hamper on the weighing machine in order to obtain the weight before dispatching it, when he heard a noise. The hamper was immediately opened, and a baby about a fortnight old was discovered wrapped in wadding, with a feeding bottle by its side. A constable was sent for, and the child was taken to the police-station. No trace of the man who left the hamper has been found.

A cutting from the *Worthing Gazette* of 11 June 1894; at the time, Oscar Wilde was holidaying with his family at Worthing. Wilde wrote *The Importance of Being Earnest* during his stay at the seaside resort, and the best-known feature of its plot clearly derives from the local newspaper's story of an abandoned baby found in a hamper that had been left at London's King's Cross station.

INTRODUCTION

WHEN Dr. Osborne first warned me of his latest literary ambition—the result of which you hold in your hands—I immediately thought, not without a touch of atypical envy: 'What a brilliant idea. Why didn't I think of that?' Then my mind flew back, as I find it increasingly does, to Melbourne, Australia, in the fifties, and to an encounter I had there with a very old English actor called Gaston Mervale, who had appeared in a touring production of *Earnest*, long whiles ago. He recounted having met Oscar Wilde in Naples, Italy, and being told by the playwright himself that he had toyed with the idea of novelizing *The Importance of Being Earnest*. Now this task has been accomplished by one of Wilde's most ardent contemporary champions, and with a wit and fluidity of writing which I am certain will have Oscar revolving with pleasure in his Père Lachaise tomb.

I cannot think of a single work for the dramatic stage, outside the Shakespeare canon, which is the source of so many helpful and felicitous quotations as this play. Now readers will be able to relish *The Importance* in the comfort of their own homes and at their own pace, without having to undertake a long journey to visit an overheated auditorium at extortionate prices, to witness, in all likelihood, an 'updated' and 'relevant' production by an all-female cast, set in fascist Italy.

Dr. Osborne has not just 'joined up the lines': he has translated the play with immense sympathy into a Handbag-sized composition much more reader-friendly than a bald theatrical script (a literary form with which even some thespians of my acquaintance have difficulty). I for one am grateful.

BARRY HUMPHRIES,
Munich, Germany, July 1999

CHAPTER
ONE

CHAPTER ONE

SUMMER came early to London in 1894. It was only the beginning of June, but already the mid-afternoon sunshine brought real warmth to the scores of stylishly dressed people strolling in Green Park. Making his way somewhat indolently through them was a young man in his mid-twenties, who paused every few yards to breathe deeply and contentedly. He seemed at peace with the world, his brown eyes surveying the passing scene calmly as he crossed the park in the direction of Piccadilly. He was a little above average height, his figure slim and shapely, his clothes well cut, and his dark brown, slightly wavy hair worn perhaps a little longer than might have been considered fashionable. His amiably handsome face wore the beginnings of a smile as he emerged from the park and crossed to the north side of Piccadilly.

His name was Algernon Moncrieff, and he was in an especially good humour on this particular morning, having just returned from a piano lesson at his music teacher's studio near Buckingham Palace on the south side of the park, a lesson at the end of which, he

3

recalled a trifle smugly, his teacher had told him that his technique was improving in leaps and bounds. In fact, what his teacher, an elderly Viennese lady, had said to him was, 'Your technique must improve. At present you are leaping and bounding all over the place.' But then, Algernon had a tendency to hear unfavourable comments as compliments. It was his way of dealing with the world.

He crossed Piccadilly, raising his hat to the young driver of a hansom cab as he nimbly skipped in front of it, and stopping to buy a green carnation from the flower-seller on the corner of Piccadilly and White Horse Street. A little further on, he turned into Half Moon Street towards his house, which was on the left-hand side at the end of the street. He rang the bell, which was immediately answered by Lane, his butler, a middle-aged man of imperturbable manner. 'Lady Bracknell and Miss Fairfax will be here shortly, Lane,' Algernon informed him. 'Would you kindly arrange afternoon tea in the morning-room, if that is not too odd a suggestion?'

'Certainly, sir,' the butler murmured as he went off towards the kitchen at the back of the house. Algernon entered the drawing-room on the right of the hallway. Seating himself at his Bösendorfer grand piano, he began to play a Chopin scherzo with great vehemence. He was still doing violence to Chopin when Lane returned from the kitchen and entered the morning-room on the other side of the hall, carrying a tray on which were cups and saucers, and a plate of neatly cut sandwiches.

When he had come to the end of his scherzo,

Algernon rose from the piano, left the room, and crossed the hall to the morning-room where Lane was setting plates out on a table.

'Did you hear what I was playing, Lane?' Algernon asked.

The butler paused, tray in hand. 'I did not think it polite to listen, sir,' he answered, his face an inscrutable mask.

Algernon smiled graciously. 'I'm sorry to hear that, for your sake,' he said. 'I don't play accurately—anyone can play accurately—but I play with wonderful expression. As far as the piano is concerned, sentiment is my forte. I keep science for life.' The word 'life' emerged from his lips as with a capital L.

'Yes, sir' was Lane's only reply, as he busied himself transferring sandwiches from a plate to an elegant silver salver.

'And,' Algernon continued, 'speaking of the science of life, have you got the cucumber sandwiches cut for Lady Bracknell?'

'Yes, sir,' the butler said, holding the salver out to Algernon as he spoke.

His employer inspected the sandwiches, took two of them, and sat down on a comfortably upholstered sofa. 'Oh, by the way, Lane,' he remarked between mouthfuls of sandwich, 'I see from your household book that on Thursday evening, when Lord Shoreman and Mr. Worthing were dining with me, eight bottles of champagne are entered as having been consumed.'

'Yes, sir,' Lane replied imperturbably. 'Eight bottles and a pint.'

'Why is it,' Algernon continued, after popping another sandwich into his mouth and munching on it greedily, 'that at a bachelor's establishment the servants invariably drink the champagne?' He licked his fingers and added hastily, 'I ask merely for information, of course.'

'I attribute it to the superior quality of the wine, sir,' Lane responded. 'I have often observed that, in married households, the champagne is rarely of a first-rate brand.'

Algernon looked startled. 'Good heavens!' he ejaculated, as he reached for another sandwich. 'Is marriage so demoralizing as that?'

The butler considered for a moment. Then he replied, 'I believe it *is* a very pleasant state, sir. I have had little experience of it myself up to the present. I have only been married once. That was in consequence of a misunderstanding between myself and a young person.'

Algernon's attention appeared to have strayed during this speech. 'I don't know that I am much interested in your family life, Lane,' he murmured languidly.

'No, sir,' Lane agreed. 'It is not a very interesting subject. I never think of it myself.'

'Very natural, I am sure,' Algernon retorted. 'That will do, Lane, thank you.'

'Thank you, sir,' the butler responded with a bow and, putting the salver on the table, he left the room.

Algernon shook his head wonderingly, at the same time reaching over to the table to take the salver in one hand and, with the other, harvest some more sandwiches. 'Lane's views on marriage,' he thought, 'seem somewhat lax.' He frowned. 'Really, if the lower orders don't set us a good example, what on earth is the use of them? They seem, as a class, to have absolutely no sense of moral responsibility.' He was still shaking his head and absent-mindedly putting another cucumber sandwich into his mouth when Lane re-entered the room, announcing, 'Mr. Ernest Worthing, sir.'

The butler was followed by a man in his late twenties who was as fair as Algernon was dark, quite as good-looking, and with the added advantage of being perhaps an inch or two taller.

Algernon greeted him warmly. 'How are you, my dear Ernest?' he cried. 'What brings you up to town?'

'Oh, pleasure, pleasure,' Ernest Worthing replied, handing his hat and cane to the butler, who took them and once more departed. 'What else should bring one anywhere?' Noticing his friend stuffing a sandwich into his mouth, he murmured, 'Eating as usual, I see, Algy.'

Algernon swallowed quickly, and replied rather stiffly, 'I believe it is customary in good society to take some slight refreshment at five o'clock.' Putting the salver back down, he asked, 'Where, my dear Ernest, have you been since last Thursday?'

'In the country,' Ernest replied off-handedly, smiling at his friend.

'What on earth do you *do* in the country?' Algernon took the liberty of wondering aloud.

Ernest shrugged his shoulders, and then began to pull his gloves off very carefully. 'When one is in town,' he replied, 'one amuses oneself. When one is in the country one amuses other people. It is excessively boring.'

'And who are the people you amuse?' Algernon asked.

'Oh, neighbours, neighbours,' his friend replied airily.

Algernon continued to probe. 'Got nice neighbours in your part of Shropshire?'

'Perfectly horrid!' said Ernest. 'Never speak to any of them.'

Algernon went to the table and took yet another sandwich. 'How immensely you must amuse them,' he commented. 'By the way,' he added, the sandwich half-way to his mouth, 'Shropshire *is* your county, is it not?'

'Eh? Shropshire? Yes, of course,' Ernest said. With a glance at the tea-table and its trappings, he added, 'Hallo! Why all these cups? Why cucumber sandwiches? Why such reckless extravagance in one so young? Who is coming to tea?'

'Oh, merely Aunt Augusta and Gwendolen,' Algernon blithely replied.

'How perfectly delighful,' Ernest exclaimed.

'Yes, that is all very well,' his friend observed, 'but I am afraid Aunt Augusta won't quite approve of your being here.'

'May I ask why?' The question seemed to have a somewhat over-innocent air to it.

'My dear fellow,' Algernon replied, attempting to introduce a stern note into his voice, 'the way you flirt with Gwendolen is perfectly disgraceful. It is almost as bad as the way Gwendolen flirts with you.'

Ernest looked aggrieved. 'I am in love with Gwendolen. I have come up to town expressly to propose to her.'

'I thought you said you had come up for pleasure,'

Algernon sighed, before adding, 'I call that business.'

'How utterly unromantic you are,' Ernest admonished him.

'I really don't see anything romantic about proposing,' Algernon said. 'It is very romantic to be in love, but there is nothing romantic about a firm proposal. Why, one may be accepted. One usually is, I believe. Then the excitement is all over. The very essence of romance is uncertainty. If ever I get married, I'll certainly try to forget the fact.'

His friend smiled acidly. 'I have no doubt about that, dear Algy,' he remarked. 'The Divorce Court was specially invented for people whose memories are so curiously constituted.'

'Oh, there is no use speculating on that subject,' said Algernon. 'Divorces are made in Heaven and—' He noticed Ernest stretching out a hand to take a sandwich, and at once moved to stop him. 'Please don't touch the cucumber sandwiches. They are ordered specially for Aunt Augusta.' He took one himself, and quickly put it into his mouth.

'Well, you have been eating them all the time,' Ernest complained.

'That is quite a different matter,' Algernon assured him. 'She is my aunt.' Taking a plate from the table, he held it out to Ernest. 'Have some bread and butter,' he offered. 'The bread and butter is for Gwendolen. Gwendolen is devoted to bread and butter.'

Ernest helped himself. 'And very good bread and butter it is, too,' he said a moment later, his mouth full.

'Well, my dear fellow,' Algernon remarked, 'you

9

need not eat as if you were going to consume it all. You behave as if you were married to her already. You are not married to her already, and I don't think you ever will be.'

Ernest paused with a piece of bread and butter partway to his mouth. 'Why on earth do you say that?'

His friend assumed a smug expression. 'Well, in the first place,' he observed, 'girls never marry the men they flirt with. They don't think it right.'

'Oh, that is nonsense,' Ernest retorted, waving his piece of bread in the air.

'It isn't,' Algernon assured him solemnly. 'It is a great truth. It accounts for the extraordinary number of bachelors that one sees all over the place.' He took another cucumber sandwich and continued, with a smirk of self-satisfaction, 'In the second place, I don't give my consent.'

'Your consent?' Ernest spluttered, attempting simultaneously to swallow another piece of bread and butter. '*Your* consent?'

Algernon smiled primly. 'My dear fellow, Gwendolen is my first cousin. And before I allow you to marry her, you will have to clear up the whole question of Cecily.'

And with that he rang the bell to summon Lane.

CHAPTER
TWO

CHAPTER TWO

W HILE he waited for the butler to appear, Algernon smiled enigmatically at Ernest. 'The whole question of Cecily,' he repeated.

'Cecily?' exclaimed Ernest, looking distinctly uncomfortable. 'Algy, what on earth do you mean by Cecily? I don't know anyone of the name of Cecily.'

Lane entered. He gave his employer a questioning look, who replied to it with a peremptory, 'Bring me that cigarette case, Lane. The one Mr. Worthing left in the smoking-room the last time he dined here.'

'Yes, sir,' Lane replied. He bowed and left the room.

'Do you mean to say,' Ernest asked his friend, 'that you have had my cigarette case all this time? I wish to goodness you had let me know. I have been writing frantic letters to Scotland Yard about it. I was very near to offering a large reward.'

'Well, I wish you would offer one,' Algernon answered. 'I happen to be more than usually hard up at the moment.'

Ernest regarded him pityingly. 'There is no point in offering a large reward now that the thing is found,' he declared.

Lane re-entered the room, holding another salver on which lay the cigarette case. Algernon took it at once, before Ernest could do so, while the butler silently retired.

'I must say, I think that is rather mean of you, Ernest,' Algernon reprimanded his friend, 'not to offer a large reward.' Opening the case, he examined it. 'However,' he continued, 'it makes no matter, for, now that I look at the inscription inside, I find that the thing isn't yours after all.'

'Of course it's mine,' Ernest insisted, coming closer to him. 'You have seen me with it a hundred times, and you have no right whatsoever to read what is written inside. It is a very ungentlemanly thing to read a private cigarette case.'

Algernon waved an arm with elegant languor. 'Oh,' he exclaimed, 'it is absurd to have a hard-and-fast rule about what one should read and what one shouldn't. More than half of modern culture depends on what one shouldn't read.'

'I am quite aware of the fact,' Ernest replied disdainfully, 'and I don't propose to discuss modern culture. It isn't the sort of thing one should talk of in private. I simply want my cigarette case back.'

'Yes, but this isn't your cigarette case,' Algernon insisted. 'This cigarette case is a present from someone of the name of Cecily, and you said you didn't know anyone of that name.'

By now Ernest was considerably exasperated. He held his hands out in front of him as though tightening them around an invisible neck, but then pulled himself together and, affecting an air of nonchalance, remarked, 'Well, if you want to know, Cecily happens to be my aunt.'

Algernon gave a snort of laughter. 'Your aunt . . .' he repeated, sounding more than a trifle sceptical.

'Yes,' replied Ernest. 'Charming old lady she is, too. Lives at Tunbridge Wells. Just give it back to me, Algy.'

Retreating behind the sofa with the cigarette case, Algernon enquired with an air of puzzlement, 'But why does she call herself "little Cecily" if she is your aunt and lives at Tunbridge Wells?' He peered closely at the inscription, and read aloud, '"From little Cecily, with her fondest love".'

Ernest came over to the sofa. Kneeling on it in front of Algernon, he exclaimed, 'My dear fellow, what on earth is there in that? Some aunts are tall, some aunts are not tall. That is a matter that surely an aunt may be allowed to decide for herself. You seem to think that every aunt should be exactly like your aunt! That is absurd. For Heaven's sake, give me back my cigarette case.'

Algernon moved away, still holding the case, and Ernest trailed after him as he stalked round the room. 'Yes,' Algernon murmured judiciously. He paused, as though wondering whether to hand over the cigarette case, but then continued, 'But why does your aunt call you her uncle? "From little Cecily, with her fondest love to her dear Uncle Jack." There is no objection, I admit, to an aunt being a small aunt, but why an aunt, no matter what her size may be, should call her own nephew her uncle, I can't quite make out. Besides, your name is not Jack at all. It is Ernest.'

'It isn't Ernest,' his friend replied quickly. 'It's Jack.'

Algernon stared at him in astonishment. 'You have always told me it was Ernest,' he exclaimed. 'I have introduced you to everyone as Ernest. You answer to the name of Ernest. You look as if your name was Ernest. In fact, you are the most earnest-looking person I ever saw in my life. It is perfectly absurd, your saying that your name isn't Ernest. It's on your cards.' He took a card from the case. 'Here is one of them. "Mr. Ernest Worthing, B.4, The Albany, London W.".' Putting the card in his pocket, he continued, 'I'll keep this as a proof that your name is Ernest if ever you attempt to deny it to me, or to Gwendolen, or to anyone else.'

Ernest had the grace to look embarrassed. Then, recovering, he said cheerfully, 'Well, my name is Ernest in town and Jack in the country, and the cigarette case was given to me in the country.'

Assuming a superior smile, Algernon shook his head. 'Yes, but that does not account for the fact that your small Aunt Cecily, who lives at Tunbridge Wells, calls you her dear uncle,' he pointed out. 'Come, old boy, you had much better have the thing out at once.'

'My dear Algy, you talk exactly as though you were a dentist,' Ernest complained. 'It is exceedingly vulgar to talk like a dentist when one is not a dentist. It produces a false impression.'

'Well, that is exactly what dentists do,' Algernon riposted, looking pleased with himself. 'Now, go on!

Tell me the whole thing. I may mention that I have always suspected you of being a confirmed and secret Bunburyist, and I am quite sure of it now.'

Ernest looked alarmed. 'Bunburyist?' he asked. 'What on earth do you mean by a Bunburyist?'

'I'll reveal to you the meaning of that incomparable expression,' Algernon replied insouciantly, 'as soon as you have been good enough to inform me why you are Ernest in town and Jack in the country.'

'Well, produce my cigarette case first.' The answer carried an unmistakable hint of truculence.

'Here it is,' said Algernon, handing him the case. 'Now produce your explanation, and pray make it improbable.' He sat down on the sofa and smiled expectantly at his friend.

'My dear fellow, there is nothing improbable about my explanation at all,' replied Ernest. 'In fact, it is perfectly ordinary. Old Mr. Thomas Cardew, who adopted me when I was a small boy, made me in his will the guardian of his grand-daughter, Miss Cecily Cardew. Cecily, who addresses me as her uncle from motives of respect that you could not possibly appreciate, lives at my place in the country under the charge of her admirable governess, Miss Prism.'

'Where is that place in the country, by the way?' Algernon asked with an innocent air.

Ernest shook his head. 'That is nothing to you, dear boy. You are not going to be invited. But I may as well tell you candidly that the place is not in Shropshire.'

'I suspected that, my dear fellow,' said Algernon. 'I have Bunburyed all over Shropshire on two separate occasions. Now, go on. Why are you Ernest in town and Jack in the country?'

Ernest paused for a moment. Then, 'My dear Algy,' he began, 'I don't know whether you will be able to understand my real motives. You are hardly serious enough.'

Since his friend merely went on looking expectant, Ernest continued. 'When one is placed in the position of guardian, one has to adopt a very high moral tone on all subjects. It's one's duty to do so. And, as a high moral tone can hardly be said to conduce very much to either one's health or one's happiness, in order to get up to town I have always pretended to have a younger brother of the name of Ernest, who lives in the Albany, and gets into the most dreadful scrapes. That, my dear Algy,' he concluded with a flourish, 'is the whole truth, pure and simple.'

'The truth, my dear Ernest,' Algernon observed, 'is rarely pure and never simple. Modern life would be very tedious if it were either, and modern literature a complete impossibility.'

'That wouldn't be at all a bad thing,' Ernest snapped. 'Modern literature—'

Algernon swiftly interrupted him. 'Literary criticism is not your forte, my dear fellow. Don't try it,' he ordered firmly. 'You should leave that kind of thing to people who haven't been at a university. They do it so well in the daily papers. What you really are is a Bunburyist. I was quite right in saying you were a Bunburyist. You are one of the most advanced Bunburyists I know.'

'What on earth do you mean?' Ernest asked, perplexed.

'Let me explain,' said Algernon. 'You have invented a very useful younger brother called Ernest, in order that you may be able to come up to town as often as you like. I have invented an extremely useful permanent invalid called Bunbury, in order that I may be able to go down into the country whenever I choose. Bunbury is perfectly invaluable. If it wasn't for Bunbury's extraordinarily bad health, for instance, I wouldn't be able to dine with you at the Café Royal tonight, for I have been engaged for more than a week to dine with Aunt Augusta.'

'But I haven't asked you to dine with me anywhere tonight,' Ernest observed mildly.

'I know,' Algernon replied. 'You are absurdly careless about sending out invitations. It is very foolish of you. Nothing annoys people so much as not receiving invitations.'

Ernest, however, was unmoved. 'You had much better dine with your Aunt Augusta,' he retorted, not without sharpness.

'I haven't the smallest intention of doing anything of the kind,' Algernon told him. 'To begin with, I dined there on Monday, and once a week is quite enough to dine with one's own relations. In the second place, whenever I do dine there I am always treated as a member of the family, and sent in to dinner with either no woman at all, or two. In the third place, I know perfectly well whom she will put me next to, tonight. She will put me next to Mary Farquhar, who always flirts with her own husband across the dinner-table. That is not very pleasant. Indeed, it is not even decent. And that sort of thing,' he observed, wagging a forefinger at his friend, 'is enormously on the increase. The number of women in London who flirt with their own husbands is perfectly scandalous. It looks so bad. It is simply washing one's clean linen in public. Besides, now that I know you to be a confirmed Bunburyist, I naturally want to talk to you about Bunburying. I want to tell you the rules.'

'But I am not a Bunburyist at all,' Ernest insisted. 'If Gwendolen accepts me'—a look of beatitude came over his face as he thought of her—'I am going to kill my brother. Indeed, I think I'll kill him in any case. Cecily is a little too much interested in him. It is rather a bore. So I am going to get rid of Ernest, one way or another. And I strongly advise you to do the same with Mr. . . . with your invalid friend who has the absurd name.'

Algernon responded with a derisive guffaw. 'Nothing,' he declared, placing his right hand over his heart, 'will induce me to part with Bunbury, and if you ever get married—which seems to me extremely problematic—you will be very glad to know Bunbury. A man who marries without knowing Bunbury has a very tedious time of it.'

'That is nonsense,' Ernest retorted hotly. 'If I marry a charming girl like Gwendolen—and she is the only girl I ever saw in my life that I would marry—I certainly won't want to know Bunbury.'

'Then your wife will,' Algernon assured him. 'You don't seem to realize, dear boy, that in married life three is company and two is none.'

'That, my dear young friend,' Ernest replied sententiously, 'is the theory that the corrupt French drama has been propounding for the last fifty years.'

'Yes. And the happy English home has proved it in half the time,' Algernon responded.

'For Heaven's sake, don't try to be cynical,' Ernest advised him irritably. 'It's perfectly easy to be cynical.'

'My dear fellow,' Algernon expostulated, 'it isn't easy to be anything nowadays. There's such a lot of beastly competition about. If only—'

He was interrupted by the sound of the door-bell being rung loud and long.

'Ah!' he exclaimed. 'That must be Aunt Augusta. Only relatives or creditors ever ring in that Wagnerian manner. Now, if I get her out of the way for ten minutes, so that you can have an opportunity to propose to Gwendolen, may I dine with you tonight at the Café Royal?'

'I suppose so, if you want to,' was his friend's somewhat ungracious reply.

'Yes. But you must be serious about it,' Algernon insisted. 'I hate people who are not serious about meals. It is so shallow of them.'

Whatever response Ernest had been about to utter, it was lost when Lane entered to announce, 'Lady Bracknell and Miss Fairfax.'

CHAPTER
THREE

CHAPTER THREE

A LGERNON altered his expression to one of welcoming cheerfulness as he went to the door to greet his relations. Lady Bracknell was an imposing *grande dame*, her posture upright, her manner formidable, and her gaze decidedly basilisk-like. Her daughter Gwendolen, who followed her into the morning-room, was an attractive, well-dressed young woman with cascading brown hair and a self-assured manner.

'Good afternoon, dear Algernon,' Lady Bracknell greeted her nephew. 'I hope you are behaving very well.'

'I am feeling very well, Aunt Augusta,' he assured her.

His aunt looked at him sternly. 'That is not,' she observed, 'quite the same thing. In fact, the two things rarely go together.' Noticing Ernest Worthing, who was hovering by the window with his eyes fixed on Gwendolen, she bowed to him coldly, but said nothing.

Algernon turned his attention to his cousin. 'Dear me, you are smart,' he exclaimed.

'I am always smart,' she replied, and to Ernest she added, 'Am I not, Mr. Worthing?'

Ernest, who had been gazing at her adoringly, declared, 'You are quite perfect, Miss Fairfax.'

This, however, was not at all what Gwendolen wanted to hear. Smiling demurely, she told him, 'Oh, I hope I am not that. It would leave no room for development, and I intend to develop in many directions.'

Her remark elicited a sigh of delight from Ernest, who gestured her to a chair. They sat down together in a corner of the room, and Lady Bracknell turned to address her nephew.

'I'm sorry if we are a little late, Algernon,' she said, 'but I was obliged to call on dear Lady Harbury. I had not been there since her poor husband's death. I never saw a woman so altered. She looks quite twenty years younger.' She gave a cluck of satisfaction at her observation, and then continued, 'Now, I think I shall have a cup of tea, and one of those nice cucumber sandwiches you promised me.'

'Certainly, Aunt Augusta,' Algernon replied, and went over to the tea-table. Lady Bracknell seated herself, and then looked across at Gwendolen, where she sat close to Ernest. 'Won't you come and sit here, Gwendolen?' she asked, an invitation to which she imparted a note of imperious command.

Gwendolen, however, was used to standing up to her mother. 'Thanks, Mamma,' she replied, 'but I'm quite comfortable where I am.'

Meanwhile, Algernon had picked up what was now an empty salver, and was gazing at it in horror.

'Good heavens, Lane!' he exclaimed. 'Why are there no cucumber sandwiches? I ordered them specially.'

With grave imperturbability, the butler, who had been pouring cups of tea, answered, 'There were no cucumbers in the market this morning, sir. I went down twice.'

'No cucumbers?'

'No, sir,' Lane replied. 'Not even for ready money.'

'That will do, Lane, thank you,' Algernon said quickly, and perhaps a trifle sharply.

'Thank you, sir,' murmured Lane as he left the room.

Algernon turned to Lady Bracknell. 'I am greatly distressed, Aunt Augusta,' he said, 'about there being no cucumbers, not even for ready money.'

She waved the apology aside. 'It really makes no matter, Algernon,' she assured him, with what, in her, passed for graciousness. 'I had some crumpets with Lady Harbury, who seems to me to be living entirely for pleasure now.'

'Yes,' Algernon agreed, with a conspiratorial smile. 'I hear her hair has turned quite gold from grief.' He went to the tea-table and began to pour the tea

His aunt positively chortled with delight at Algernon's witticism. 'Her hair has certainly changed its colour,' she affirmed. 'From what cause I, of course, cannot say.'

Algernon handed Lady Bracknell a cup of tea. 'Thank you,' she said, inclining her head graciously. 'Now, Algernon,' she continued, 'I've quite a treat for you tonight. I am going to send you in to dinner with Mary Farquhar. She is such a nice woman, and so attentive to her husband. It's delightful to watch them.'

Taking care not to catch Ernest's eye, Algernon looked grave. 'I am afraid, Aunt Augusta, that I shall have to give up the pleasure of dining with you tonight after all.'

Lady Bracknell frowned. 'I hope not, Algernon. It would put my table completely out. Your uncle would have to dine upstairs.' She thought for a moment and then conceded, 'Fortunately he is accustomed to that.'

'It is a great bore,' Algernon sighed, 'and, I need hardly say, a terrible disappointment to me, but the fact is I have just had a telegram to say that my poor friend Bunbury is very ill again.' He glanced apprehensively at Ernest as he mentioned Bunbury, but that young man and Gwendolen were gazing silently into each other's eyes. 'Poor Bunbury's nurse seems to think I should be with him.'

'It is very strange,' Lady Bracknell remarked. 'This Mr. Bunbury seems to suffer from curiously bad health.'

'Yes,' Algernon agreed. 'Poor old Bunbury is a dreadful invalid.'

Lady Bracknell fixed her nephew with one of her most intimidating glares. 'Well, I must say, Algernon,' she announced, 'that I think it is high time that Mr. Bunbury made up his mind whether he was going to live or to die. This shilly-shallying with the question is absurd.'

'But, really, Aunt Augusta—' Algernon began.

His aunt held up a hand for silence. 'Nor do I in any way approve of the modern sympathy with invalids.

I consider it morbid. Illness of any kind is hardly a thing to be encouraged in others. Health is—'

Algernon attempted to interrupt, but his aunt flashed another intimidating glance at him and went on, 'Health, I was about to say, is the primary duty of life. I am always telling that to your poor uncle, but he never seems to take much notice, as far as any improvement in his ailment goes.'

'I am sorry to hear that, Aunt Augusta,' Algernon murmured sympathetically, 'but—'

Again Lady Bracknell held up a hand for silence. 'In any case, I should be much obliged,' she instructed her nephew, 'if you would ask Mr. Bunbury, from me, to be kind enough not to have a relapse on Saturday, for I rely on you to arrange my music for me on that evening. It is my last reception of the season, and one wants something that will encourage conversation, particularly now at the end of the season when everyone has practically said whatever they had to say, which, in most cases, was probably not much.'

'I'll speak to Bunbury, Aunt Augusta,' Algernon assured her. 'That is, of course, if he is still conscious. But, assuming that he is, I think I can promise you that he'll be all right by Saturday. Of course, the music for your reception presents a great difficulty. You see, if one plays good music, people don't listen, and if one plays bad music, people don't talk.'

His aunt made an impatient gesture, at which Algernon hastened to reassure her. 'I'm sure we can choose something suitable,' he declared. 'Actually, I'd like to run over the programme I've drawn out, if you will kindly come into the next room for a moment.'

'Thank you, Algernon. It is very thoughtful of you,' Lady Bracknell replied as she rose to follow him. 'I am sure the programme will be delightful—after a few expurgations, of course.' She stood still for a moment, before continuing, 'French songs I cannot possibly allow. People always seem to think that they are improper, and either look shocked, which is vulgar, or laugh, which is worse. But German sounds a thoroughly respectable language, and indeed I believe is so.' She looked around at her daughter. 'Gwendolen, you will accompany me.'

Gwendolen had long ago arrived at a method of accommodating her mother. 'Certainly, Mamma,' she replied submissively, but she remained behind with Ernest as Algernon escorted Lady Bracknell into the drawing-room.

Silence reigned in the morning-room after their departure. For a moment or two, Ernest and Gwendolen simply gazed at each other without speaking, and then Ernest rose and walked to the window. He looked out at the street for a few seconds, before turning to address her. 'What a charming day it has been, Miss Fairfax,' he observed.

'Pray don't talk to me about the weather, Mr. Worthing,' Gwendolen replied. 'Whenever people talk to me about the weather, I always feel quite certain that they mean something else. And that makes me so nervous.'

'I do mean something else,' he admitted.

'I thought so,' Gwendolen declared. 'In fact, I am never wrong.'

'And,' Ernest continued, 'I would like to be allowed to take advantage of Lady Bracknell's temporary absence—'

'Indeed, I would advise you to do so,' Gwendolen interrupted, with a certain urgency in her tone. 'Mamma has a way of coming back suddenly into a room that I have often had to speak to her about.'

Ernest cast an involuntary look at the door, then continued, 'Miss Fairfax, ever since I met you, I have admired you more than any girl ... I have ever met since ... I met you.'

Gwendolen looked at him with complacence. 'Yes, I am quite well aware of the fact,' she assured him. 'And I often wish that, in public at any rate, you had been more demonstrative. For me, you have always had an irresistible fascination. Even before I met you, I was far from indifferent to you.'

The remark caused Ernest to stare at her in amazement. He was about to speak when she stopped him with a gesture which reminded him, disconcertingly, of her mother. 'We live, as I hope you know, Mr. Worthing,' she said, 'in an age of ideals. The fact is constantly mentioned in the more expensive monthly magazines, and has reached the provincial pulpits, I am told. My ideal has always been to love someone of the name of Ernest. There is something in that name that inspires absolute confidence. The moment Algernon first mentioned to me that he had a friend called Ernest, I knew I was destined to love you.'

Ernest continued to stare at her, a wondering expression on his face. 'You really love me, Gwendolen?' he exclaimed.

'Passionately,' she responded, gazing at him in rapt adoration.

'Darling!' he cried. 'You don't know how happy you've made me.'

'My own Ernest!' Gwendolen responded.

They embraced. Then, holding her at arm's length, Ernest enquired tentatively, 'But ... ah ... you don't ... you don't really mean to say that you couldn't love me if my name wasn't Ernest?'

'But your name *is* Ernest,' she replied with a laugh.

'Yes, I know it is,' he responded hurriedly. 'But supposing it was something else? Do you mean to say you couldn't love me then?'

Gwendolen looked puzzled. Then her face brightened. 'Ah, that is clearly a metaphysical speculation,' she said, 'and like most metaphysical speculations has very little reference at all to the actual facts of real life, as we know them.'

Ernest frowned worriedly. 'Personally, darling, to speak quite candidly,' he persisted, 'I don't much care for the name of Ernest. In fact, I don't think it suits me at all.'

'Nonsense,' Gwendolen declared. 'It suits you perfectly. It is a divine name. It has a music of its own. It produces vibrations.'

'Well, really, Gwendolen,' he expostulated, 'I must say that I think there are lots of other much nicer names.' He gestured vaguely, and then said, 'I think Jack, for instance, is a particularly charming name.'

'Jack?' Gwendolen's tone was dismissive. 'No, there is very little music in the name Jack, if any at all. It does not thrill. It produces absolutely no vibrations.' Warming to her theme, she went on, 'I have known several Jacks, and they all, without exception, were more than usually plain. Besides, Jack is a notorious vulgarism for John! And I pity any woman who is married to a man called John. She would probably never be allowed to know the entrancing pleasure of a single moment's solitude. No,' she concluded, 'the only really safe name is Ernest.'

'Gwendolen,' Ernest got out hurriedly, 'I must get christened at once—I mean we must get married at once. There is no time to be lost.'

Gwendolen looked extremely surprised. 'Married, Mr. Worthing?' she asked, as though she did not know the meaning of the word.

Ernest was astounded. 'Well . . . surely,' he stammered. 'You know that I love you, and you led me to believe, Miss Fairfax, that you were not absolutely indifferent to me.'

'I adore you,' she admitted happily. 'But you haven't proposed to me yet. Nothing has been said at all about marriage.' As he continued to gaze at her uncomprehendingly, she declared with emphasis, 'The subject has not even been touched on.' She turned away and sat down.

'Well,' said Ernest, still unsure of his ground, 'may I propose to you now?'

'I think it would be an admirable opportunity,' Gwendolen assured him. 'And to spare you any possible disappointment, Mr. Worthing, I think it only fair to tell you quite frankly beforehand that I am fully determined to accept you.'

'Gwendolen!' he shouted joyously.

She remained calm and self-possessed. 'Yes, Mr. Worthing,' she responded, 'what have you got to say to me?'

'You know what I've got to say to you,' Ernest replied, perplexed.

'Yes, but you don't say it,' she pointed out, with a touch of asperity.

At last he understood her meaning. 'Gwendolen,' he declared, going down on his knees before her, 'will you marry me?'

'Of course I will, darling,' she assured him. 'How long you have been about it! I am afraid you have had very little experience in how to propose.'

Ernest looked shocked. 'My own one,' he exclaimed, 'I have never loved anyone in the world but you.'

'Yes, but men often propose for practice,' observed Gwendolen. 'I know my brother Gerald does. All my friends tell me so.' She gazed at him with affection. 'What wonderfully blue eyes you have, Ernest. They are quite, quite blue.'

He returned her gaze adoringly.

'I hope you will always look at me just like that,' she murmured tenderly, 'especially when there are other people present.'

The door opened suddenly, and Lady Bracknell swept

into the room. She looked appalled by the sight that met her eyes.

'Mr. Worthing!' she exclaimed. 'Rise, sir, from this semi-recumbent posture. It is most indecorous.'

'Mamma!' Gwendolen cried indignantly. Ernest tried to rise, but she restrained him. 'I must beg you to retire, Mamma,' she continued. 'This is no place for you. Besides, Mr. Worthing has not quite finished yet.'

'Finished what, may I ask?' Lady Bracknell asked magisterially.

The young couple rose to their feet together. 'I am engaged to Mr. Worthing, Mamma,' Gwendolen told her mother.

'Pardon me,' replied Lady Bracknell with icy dignity, 'but you are not engaged to anyone. When you do become engaged to someone, I—or your father, should his health permit him—will inform you of the fact. An engagement should come on a young girl as a surprise, pleasant or unpleasant, as the case may be. It is hardly a matter that she could be allowed to arrange for herself.'

Her ladyship stared at Ernest haughtily. 'And now,' she continued, 'I have a few questions to put to you, Mr. Worthing. While I am making these enquiries, you, Gwendolen, will wait for me outside in the carriage.'

'Mamma!' Gwendolen reproved her, outraged.

'In the carriage, Gwendolen!' her mother insisted.

Gwendolen paused, then walked with dignity to the door. She and Ernest blew kisses to each other behind

Lady Bracknell's back, the sound of which caused that lady to look vaguely about, as if wondering what the noise was. When she turned around, Gwendolen was still at the door. 'Gwendolen,' Lady Bracknell repeated imperiously, 'the carriage.'

'Yes, Mamma,' Gwendolen replied resignedly, and as she left the room she directed a final backward look of affection at Ernest.

CHAPTER
FOUR

CHAPTER FOUR

AFTER Gwendolen had left, Lady Bracknell went to the most comfortable chair in the room, and sat down. 'You may take a seat, Mr. Worthing,' she said to Ernest as she scrutinized him haughtily.

'Thank you, Lady Bracknell, I prefer standing,' he replied politely.

Lady Bracknell searched in her capacious pocket for a note-book and pencil. When she had them in her hand, she looked up at Ernest again. 'I feel bound to tell you,' she said, 'that you are not down on my list of eligible young men, although I have the same list as the dear Duchess of Bolton has. We work together, in fact. However, I am quite ready to enter your name, should your answers be what a really affectionate mother requires.' Her expression seemed to indicate that the likelihood of his name being added to her list was extremely remote. 'Do you smoke?' she asked.

'Well, yes,' Ernest replied, 'I must admit I smoke.'

Lady Bracknell looked somewhat surprised and even pleased at this answer. 'I am glad to hear it,' she said.

'A man should always have an occupation of some kind. There are far too many idle men in London as it is.' She wrote in her note-book, and then looked up. 'How old are you?' she enquired.

'I am twenty-nine,' Ernest answered.

'A very good age to be married at,' Lady Bracknell observed, as she made a note of it in her book. She looked at him thoughtfully, and then added, 'I have always been of the opinion that a man who desires to get married should know either everything or nothing. Which do you know?'

Ernest considered for a few seconds before replying suavely, 'I know nothing, Lady Bracknell.'

'I am pleased to hear it,' she declared. 'I do not approve of anything that tampers with natural ignorance. Ignorance is like a delicate, exotic fruit. Touch it, and the bloom is gone. The whole theory of modern education is radically unsound. Fortunately, in England at any rate, education produces no effect whatsoever.' She looked at Ernest to make sure that he was paying full attention to her words. 'If it did, education would prove a serious danger to the upper classes, and probably lead to acts of violence in Grosvenor Square.' She thought for a moment, her pencil poised, before asking, 'What is your income?'

'Between seven and eight thousand a year,' Ernest informed her.

Again Lady Bracknell looked pleased. She made another note in her book, and then looked up again. 'Is that in land, or in investments?'

'In investments, chiefly,' Ernest replied.

'That is satisfactory,' she conceded. 'What between the duties expected of one during one's lifetime, and the duties exacted from one after one's death, land has ceased to be either a profit or a pleasure. It gives one position, and prevents one from keeping it up.' She gave a small hiss of derision. 'That's all that can be said about land.'

Ernest was more than a trifle bemused by this observation. With a deprecatory gesture, he admitted, 'I do have a country house—with some land, of course, attached to it. About fifteen hundred acres, I believe. But I don't depend on that for my real income.' Thinking that perhaps a lighter touch might be called for, he added, 'In fact, as far as I can make out, the poachers are the only people who make anything out of it.'

Lady Bracknell ignored his attempt at levity. 'A country house!' she exclaimed. 'How many bedrooms?' Without waiting for a reply, she murmured, as though to herself, 'Well, that point can be cleared up afterwards.' Once more she wrote in her book, and then addressed Ernest again. 'You have a town house, I hope? A girl with a simple, unspoiled nature like Gwendolen could hardly be expected to reside in the country.'

'Well, I own a house in Belgrave Square, but it is let by the year to Lady Bloxham. Of course, I can get it back whenever I like, at six months' notice.'

'Lady Bloxham?' From her expression, it was evident that Gwendolen's mother did not care for the sound of the name. 'I don't know her.'

'Oh, she goes about very little. She is a lady considerably advanced in years.'

'Ah, nowadays that is no guarantee of respectability of character,' Lady Bracknell responded. Plainly, Ernest was not going to gain her favour so easily. Her pencil again poised above her note-book, she enquired, 'What number in Belgrave Square?'

'One hundred and forty-nine.'

Lady Bracknell shook her head. 'The unfashionable side,' she observed. 'I thought there was something. However, that could easily be altered.'

Ernest made another attempt at humour. 'Do you mean the fashion, or the side?' he asked, with what he intended to be an ingratiating smile.

'Both, if necessary, I presume,' Lady Bracknell replied sternly. She looked at him grimly, as another area of enquiry suddenly occurred to her. 'What are your politics?' she asked, her intonation making it clear that she expected the worst.

'Well, I must admit I really have none,' Ernest explained. 'I am a Liberal.'

She was relieved. 'Oh, they count as Tories,' she said. 'They dine with us. Or come in the evening, at any rate.' She consulted her note-book, and then continued, 'Now to minor matters. Are your parents living?'

'I'm afraid I have lost both my parents,' Ernest replied.

Lady Bracknell looked displeased. 'To lose one parent, Mr. Worthing,' she reproved him, 'may be regarded as a misfortune. To lose both, however, looks like carelessness.'

Poor Ernest could think of no suitable response. Fortunately, none was required, for Lady Bracknell immediately went on, 'Who was your father? He was evidently a man of some wealth. Was he born in what the radical papers call the purple of commerce, or did he rise from the ranks of the aristocracy?'

'I am afraid I really don't know,' Ernest admitted. 'The fact is, Lady Bracknell, I said I had lost my parents. It would be nearer the truth to say that my parents seem to have lost me.'

He paused. Lady Bracknell regarded him with suspicion as he continued, 'I don't actually know who I am by birth. I was . . . well, I was found.'

'*Found?*' she exclaimed. The look of incredulity on her face was almost comical.

Ernest hastened to explain. 'The late Mr. T-Thomas C-Cardew,' he stammered nervously, 'an old gentleman of a very charitable and kindly disposition, found me. He gave me the name of Worthing, because he happened to have a first-class ticket for Worthing in his pocket at the time.' Ernest paused to see how this information was received, and then added, 'Worthing is a place in Sussex. It is a seaside resort.'

Lady Bracknell fixed him with her basilisk stare. 'Where did the charitable gentleman who had a first-class ticket for this seaside resort find you?'

Ernest looked grave. 'In a hand-bag,' he replied solemnly.

'A *hand-bag?*' Lady Bracknell made it sound as though he had mentioned something obscene.

Ernest's tone was very serious as he explained, 'Yes, Lady Bracknell. I was in a hand-bag—a somewhat large, black leather hand-bag, with handles to it—an ordinary hand-bag, in fact.'

She seemed, momentarily, at a loss, but rallied to ask, 'In what locality did this Mr. James, or Thomas, Cardew, come across this ordinary hand-bag?'

'In the cloak-room at Victoria Station,' Ernest replied. As she looked both horrified and incredulous, he added hastily, 'It was given to him in mistake for his own.'

'The cloak-room at Victoria Station!' Lady Bracknell echoed, in tones that made it sound a most insalubrious location.

'Yes,' said Ernest, adding helpfully, 'The Brighton line.'

'The line is immaterial,' Lady Bracknell declared, dismissively. She looked about the room as if seeking aid. Finding none, she addressed Ernest again. 'Mr. Worthing, I confess I feel somewhat bewildered by what you have just told me. To be born, or at any rate bred, in a hand-bag, whether it had handles or not, seems to me to display a contempt for the ordinary decencies of family life that reminds one of the worst excesses of the French Revolution. And I presume you know what *that* unfortunate movement led to?'

Receiving no answer from Ernest, who merely contemplated her miserably, she continued, 'As for the particular locality in which the hand-bag was found, a cloakroom at a railway station might serve to conceal a social indiscretion—has probably, indeed, been used for that purpose before now—but it could hardly be regarded as an assured basis for a recognized position in good society.'

Ernest could see that his chances of marrying Gwendolen were lessening minute by minute. He decided to fling himself on Lady Bracknell's mercy.

'May I ask you then,' he implored her, 'what you would advise me to do? I need hardly say I would do anything in the world to ensure Gwendolen's happiness.'

Lady Bracknell replaced the note-book and pencil firmly in her pocket. 'I would strongly advise you, Mr. Worthing,' she said icily, 'to try and acquire some relations as soon as possible, and to make a definite effort to produce at any rate one parent, of either sex, before the season is quite over.'

'Well, I don't see how I could possibly manage to do that,' Ernest admitted in desperation. 'I can produce the hand-bag at any time. It is in my dressing-room at home. I really think that should satisfy you, Lady Bracknell.'

'*Me*, sir?' she expostulated. 'What has it to do with me? You can hardly imagine that I and Lord Bracknell would dream of allowing our only daughter—a girl brought up with the utmost care—to marry into a cloakroom, and form an alliance with a parcel.'

And uttering a glacial 'Goodbye, Mr. Worthing', Lady Bracknell sailed out of the room in majestic indignation.

'Goodbye,' Ernest found himself saying to the door, which she had slammed shut behind her.

CHAPTER
FIVE

CHAPTER FIVE

A s Ernest stood looking miserably at the door through which Lady Bracknell had departed, taking with her his hopes of happiness, the strains of Mendelssohn's Wedding March could be heard, banged out enthusiastically by Algernon on the piano in the drawing-room. Ernest went to the door and shouted furiously, 'For goodness' sake, don't play that ghastly tune, Algy! How idiotic you are!'

The music stopped abruptly in mid-phrase. Ernest retreated to the centre of the morning room, still furious, and a moment later Algernon entered. 'Didn't it go off all right, old boy?' he asked cheerfully.

Ernest said nothing, but merely glared at him.

'You don't mean to say Gwendolen refused you?' Algernon enquired. 'I know it is a way she has. She is always refusing people who propose. I think it is most ill-natured of her.'

Ernest's expression changed from anger to gloom. 'Oh, Gwendolen is as right as rain,' he said. 'As far as she is concerned, we are engaged. But her mother is perfectly unbearable. I've never met such a Gorgon.'

He paused for a moment, and then continued, 'I don't really know what a Gorgon is like, but I am quite sure that Lady Bracknell is one. In any case, she is a monster without being a myth, which is rather unfair.' He suddenly remembered his manners. 'I beg your pardon, Algy, I suppose I shouldn't talk about your own aunt in that way to you.'

'My dear boy,' his friend replied, 'I love hearing my relations abused. It is the only thing that makes me put up with them at all. Relations are simply a tedious pack of people who haven't got the remotest knowledge of how to live, nor the smallest instinct about when to die.'

'Oh, that is nonsense,' Ernest retorted.

'It isn't,' Algernon insisted.

'Well, I won't argue about the matter,' said Ernest. 'You always want to argue about things.'

'That is exactly what things were originally made for,' Algernon replied smugly.

'Upon my word,' Ernest declared, 'if I thought that, I'd shoot myself.' Then another notion struck him. 'You don't think,' he asked Algernon, 'that there is any chance of Gwendolen becoming like her mother in about a hundred and fifty years, do you, Algy?'

'All women become like their mothers,' replied Algernon. 'That is their tragedy. No man does. That's his.'

Ernest assumed a bored expression. 'Is that clever?' he asked superciliously.

'It is perfectly phrased,' Algernon replied, 'and quite as true as any observation in civilized life should be.'

Ernest uttered a groan of exasperation. 'I am sick to death of cleverness,' he said irritably. 'Everybody is clever nowadays.' He looked about him, as though surrounded by everybody. 'You can't go anywhere without meeting clever people. The thing has become an absolute public nuisance.' He looked around the room again, this time more desperately. 'I wish to goodness we had a few fools left,' he exclaimed.

'We have,' Algernon assured him.

'I should very much like to meet them,' came the heartfelt rejoinder. 'What do they talk about, I wonder?'

'The fools? Oh, about the clever people, of course,' said Algernon.

'Really? What fools,' Ernest murmured, losing interest in the subject.

Algernon contemplated his friend for a moment, before asking, 'By the way, did you tell Gwendolen the truth about your being Ernest in town, and Jack in the country?'

'My dear fellow,' Ernest replied in his most patronizing manner, 'the truth isn't quite the sort of thing one tells to a nice, sweet, refined girl. What extraordinary ideas you have about the way to behave to a woman!'

'The only way to behave to a woman,' Algernon announced with authority, 'is to make love to her, if she is pretty, and to someone else, if she is plain.'

'Oh, that is nonsense,' Ernest snorted dismissively. He turned away and walked to the table, intending to seek solace in whatever food might be left.

'But,' asked Algernon, a gleam of amusement in his eyes, 'what are you going to do about your brother?

What will happen to the profligate Ernest?'

Ernest shrugged his shoulders. 'Oh, before the end of the week I shall have got rid of him,' he declared. 'I'll say he died in Paris of apoplexy. Lots of people die of apoplexy, quite suddenly, don't they?'

'Yes,' Algernon agreed, 'but it's usually hereditary, my dear fellow. It's a sort of thing that runs in families. You had much better say a severe chill.'

Ernest regarded his friend anxiously. 'You are sure a severe chill isn't hereditary, or anything of that kind,' he asked.

'Of course it isn't,' Algernon assured him.

'Very well, then,' replied Ernest. He sounded quite determined. 'My poor brother Ernest is carried off suddenly, in Paris, by a severe chill. That gets rid of him.'

Algernon, however, wished to pursue the matter a little further. 'But,' he observed, ' I thought you said that your ward, Miss—what is her name, Miss Cardew?—I thought you said that she had become a little too much interested in your poor brother Ernest. Won't she feel his loss a good deal?'

'Oh, that is all right,' Ernest said with confidence. 'Cecily is not a silly romantic girl, I am glad to say. She has got a capital appetite, she goes for long walks, and she pays no attention at all to her lessons.'

Algernon nodded approvingly. 'I would rather like to meet Cecily,' he observed.

'I will take very good care to see that you never do,' Ernest declared in a most heartfelt manner. 'She is excessively pretty, and she is only just eighteen.'

Algernon's expression became even more approving. Then, with a mischievous glint in his eye, he asked innocently, 'Have you told Gwendolen yet that you have an excessively pretty ward who is only just eighteen?'

His friend gave him a pitying look. 'Oh, one doesn't blurt these things out to people,' he replied. 'Cecily and Gwendolen are perfectly certain to be extremely great friends. I'll bet you anything you like that, half an hour after they have met, they will be calling each other "sister".'

'Women only do that,' Algernon said, 'when they have called each other a lot of other things first.' Changing the subject abruptly, he continued, 'Now, my dear boy, if we want to get a good table at the Café Royal, we really must go and dress. Do you know it is nearly seven?'

'Oh, it is always nearly seven,' said Ernest irritably, his mind doubtless still engaged with his problems of romance.

'Well, I'm hungry,' Algernon complained.

'I never knew you when you weren't,' Ernest snapped.

'What shall we do after dinner?' Algernon asked. 'Go to a theatre?'

'Oh, no. I loathe listening to things,' Ernest replied.

'Well, shall we go to the club?'

'Oh, no. I hate talking to people.'

'Well then, we might perhaps trot round to the Empire at ten?'

'Oh, no. I can't bear looking at things. It is so silly.'

'Well, what shall we do?'

'Nothing,' said Ernest, decisively.

'It is awfully hard work doing nothing,' Algernon complained. 'However, I don't mind hard work where there is no definite object of any kind.'

Ernest looked exasperated. He was about to speak, when Lane came into the room and announced, 'Miss Fairfax.' He stood aside to let Gwendolen enter, and then left.

'Gwendolen, upon my word!' her cousin greeted her.

'Algy, kindly turn your back,' Gwendolen ordered. 'I have something very particular to say to Mr. Worthing.'

'Really, Gwendolen,' said Algernon reprovingly, 'I don't think I can allow this at all.'

'Algy, you always adopt a strictly immoral attitude towards life,' she retorted. 'You are not quite old enough to do that.'

With a graceful shrug of the shoulders and an ironic little bow, Algernon retired to the fireplace.

'My own darling!' Ernest exclaimed, rushing forward to embrace Gwendolen.

She kept him at a distance. 'Ernest,' she said, 'we may never be married. From the expression on Mamma's face, I fear we never shall.'

He was about to speak, but she held up a hand for silence, and continued, 'Few parents nowadays pay any regard to what their children say to them. The old-fashioned respect for the young is fast dying out. Whatever influence I ever had over Mamma, I lost at the age of three. But although she may prevent us from becoming man and wife, and I may marry someone else, and indeed may marry often, nothing that she can possibly do will alter my eternal devotion to you.'

'Dear Gwendolen!' Ernest cried. He would have continued, but again she prevented him.

'The story of your romantic origin,' she assured him, 'as related to me by Mamma with unpleasing comments, has naturally stirred the deeper fibres of my nature. Your Christian name has an irresistible fascination. The simplicity of your character makes you exquisitely incomprehensible to me.' Without a pause, she moved on to more practical matters. 'Your town address at the Albany I have. What is your address in the country?'

'The Manor House, Woolton, Hertfordshire,' Ernest told her hastily.

Algernon, who had been carefully, if surreptitiously, listening, smiled to himself and, unnoticed by the young lovers, wrote the address on his shirt-cuff. Then, turning to the bookshelves, he selected a copy of the Railway Guide and began to peruse it.

Gwendolen, meanwhile, asked Ernest, 'There is a good postal service, I suppose? It may be necesssary to do something desperate. That, of course, will require serious consideration. I will communicate with you daily.'

'My own one!' Ernest exclaimed romantically, though somewhat fatuously.

Gwendolen, however, remained practical. 'How long do you remain in town?'

'Till Monday, my dearest dear.'

'Good.' Still gazing at Ernest, she called graciously to Algernon. 'Algy, you may turn around now.'

'Thanks, I've turned around already,' he replied, as indeed he had.

'You may also ring the bell,' Gwendolen added.

Algernon did as he was told.

'You will let me see you to your carriage, my own darling?' asked Ernest.

'Certainly, my dearest,' she replied.

Ernest turned to Lane, who had just entered the room with several letters on a salver, and said, 'I shall see Miss Fairfax out.' He and Gwendolen left, as Lane presented the letters to Algernon. After glancing at the envelopes, he tore them all up, assuming them to be bills. 'A glass of sherry, I think, Lane,' he said.

'Yes, sir,' the butler replied, going to the decanter.

'Tomorrow, Lane,' Algernon added after a moment, 'I shall be engaged in Bunburying.'

'Yes, sir,' said Lane.

'I shall probably not be back until Monday,' Algernon continued. 'You can put out my dress clothes, my smoking jacket, and all the Bunbury suits.'

'Yes, sir,' Lane murmured, handing his employer a glass of sherry.

'I hope tomorrow will be a fine day, Lane,' Algernon continued, breezily.

'It never is, sir,' the butler replied.

'Lane, you're a perfect pessimist.'

'I do my best to give satisfaction, sir.' He bowed and left the room, as Ernest re-entered.

'Now, there's a sensible, intellectual girl,' said Ernest. 'The only girl I ever cared for in my life.'

Algernon laughed immoderately, at which Ernest looked affronted. 'What on earth are you so amused at?' he demanded.

'Oh, I'm a little anxious about poor Bunbury, that is all,' Algernon assured him.

Ernest, recovering his equanimity, regarded his friend affectionately. 'You know, Algy, if you don't take care, your friend Bunbury will get you into a serious scrape some day.'

'I love scrapes,' Algernon declared. 'They are the only things that are never serious.'

'Oh, that's nonsense, Algy. You never talk anything but nonsense.'

'Nobody ever does,' Algernon retorted.

Ernest looked indignantly at him, and left the room without another word. Algernon watched him go, then lit a cigarette, read the address on his shirt-cuff, and allowed a self-satisfied smile to appear on his face.

CHAPTER
SIX

CHAPTER SIX

THE country house whose address Ernest Worthing—to give him his town name—had imparted to Gwendolen was a manor house set in delightful countryside, in the county of Hertfordshire some twenty miles from London, all undulating hills and green fields. On the morning of the day following Ernest's unhappy interview with Lady Bracknell, Cecily Cardew, the ward of Jack Worthing—to give him his country name—was in the garden with her governess, Miss Prism. It was a fine Saturday morning, and the sun was shining brightly. The garden, an old-fashioned one, was full of roses, among which Cecily, an attractive, fair-haired young lady of eighteen, was wandering about with a watering-can. Not far from the grey stone steps that led up to the house, Miss Prism, a middle-aged woman of prim demeanour, sat at a round table under the shade of a large yew tree. The table was surrounded by basketwork chairs and covered with books.

'Cecily! Cecily!' Miss Prism called. 'Surely such a utilitarian occupation as the watering of flowers is rather the gardener's duty than yours? Especially at a moment when intellectual pleasures await you.' With an impatient look, she gestured to the books in front of her. 'Your German grammar is on the table. Pray come here and open it at page fifteen. We will repeat yesterday's lesson.'

Cecily put down her watering-can and, very slowly and reluctantly, came over to the table. 'But I don't like German,' she protested, pouting slightly. 'It isn't at all a becoming language. I know perfectly well that I look quite plain after my German lesson.'

Miss Prism dismissed this excuse with a vigorous shake of her head. 'Child,' she declared, 'you know how anxious your guardian is that you should improve yourself in every way. He laid particular stress on your German as he was leaving for town yesterday. Indeed, he always lays stress on your German when he is leaving for town.'

At the thought of her guardian, an affectionate smile lit up Cecily's face. 'Dear Uncle Jack is so very serious!' she exclaimed. 'Sometimes he is so serious that I think he cannot be quite well.'

Miss Prism drew herself up. 'Your guardian enjoys the best of health,' she told Cecily repressively. 'His gravity of demeanour is especially to be commended in one so comparatively young as he is. I know no one who has a higher sense of duty and responsibility.'

'I suppose,' Cecily returned thoughtfully, 'that is why he often looks a little bored when we three are together.'

'Cecily!' Miss Prism admonished her, 'I am surprised at you. Mr. Worthing has many troubles in his life.

Idle merriment and triviality would be out of place in his conversation.' Then, as the girl seated herself at the table, her governess tapped her on the arm. 'You must remember,' she said severely, 'Mr. Worthing's constant anxiety about that unfortunate young man, his brother.'

Cecily brightened. 'I wish Uncle Jack would allow that unfortunate young man, his brother, to come down here sometimes,' she said. 'We might have a good influence over him, Miss Prism. I am sure *you* certainly would.'

Miss Prism seemed struck by this, and Cecily hastened to press home her advantage. 'After all,' she continued, 'you know German, and geology, and things of that kind influence a man very much.' She opened one of the books on the table and began to write in it.

Shaking her head regretfully, Miss Prism murmured, 'I do not think that even I could produce any effect on a character that according to his own brother's admission is irretrievably weak and vacillating.' After reflecting for a moment, she added, 'Indeed, I am not sure that I would desire to reclaim him. I am not in favour of this modern mania for turning bad people into good people at a moment's notice. As a man sows, so let him reap.' Noticing that Cecily was paying no attention to her but was busily writing, she rapped on the table. 'You must put away your diary, Cecily. I really don't see why you should keep a diary at all.'

Cecily looked up from the book and flashed a sunny smile at her governess. 'I keep a diary in order to enter the wonderful secrets of my life,' she said. 'If I didn't write them down, I should probably forget all about them.'

Miss Prism wagged an admonitory finger at the girl. 'Memory, my dear Cecily,' she declared, 'is the diary that we all carry about with us.'

'Yes,' said Cecily, 'but it usually chronicles the things that have never happened, and couldn't possibly have happened.' Warming to her theme, she continued, 'I believe that memory is responsible for nearly all the three-volume novels that fill up the libraries.'

Miss Prism bridled. 'Do not speak slightingly of the three-volume novel, Cecily,' she said. 'I wrote one myself in earlier days.'

'Did you really, Miss Prism?' asked Cecily admiringly. 'How wonderfully clever you are. I hope it did not end happily. I don't like novels that end happily. They depress me so much.'

'The good ended happily, and the bad unhappily,' said Miss Prism. 'That is what Fiction means.'

Cecily took a moment to digest this information. 'I suppose so,' she said. 'But it seems very unfair.' She briefly contemplated the unfairness of the situation, and then enquired, 'Was your novel ever published?'

'Alas, no,' Miss Prism replied, sadly. 'The manuscript unfortunately was abandoned.' Cecily gave a start of surprise, and her governess hastened to explain that she had used the word 'abandoned' in the sense of being lost or mislaid, and not as a description of the work. 'But, return to your work, child,' she said. 'These speculations are profitless.'

Cecily, however, had noticed someone approaching. With an arch smile she exclaimed, 'Oh, look, Miss Prism. I see dear Dr. Chasuble coming into the garden.'

Miss Prism seemed a trifle flustered at this. But she rose to greet the visitor and, as he neared them, advanced towards him with hand outstretched. 'Dr. Chasuble!' she exclaimed. 'This is indeed a pleasure.'

The Reverend Canon Chasuble, Doctor of Divinity, a portly, round-faced, balding man in his sixties, was puffing and mopping his brow as he approached the ladies at a stately pace.

'And how are we this morning?' he greeted them, adding, 'Miss Prism, you are, I trust, well?'

Before the governess could answer, Cecily said, 'Miss Prism has just been complaining of a slight headache. I think it would do her so much good to have a short stroll with you in the park, Dr. Chasuble.'

'Cecily,' Miss Prism objected, looking puzzled, 'I have not mentioned anything about a headache.'

'No, dear Miss Prism, I know that,' her pupil replied glibly. 'But I felt instinctively that you had a headache. Indeed, I was thinking about that, and not about my German lesson, when Dr. Chasuble arrived.'

'I hope you are not inattentive, Cecily,' the Rector said reprovingly, with a covert glance at Miss Prism.

'I am afraid I am,' was Cecily's demure reply.

'That is strange,' he observed. 'Were I fortunate enough to be Miss Prism's pupil, I would hang upon her lips.'

This remark elicited a look of shock from the governess, causing Dr. Chasuble to add hurriedly, 'I spoke metaphorically, of course. My metaphor was drawn from bees.' Waving an arm in the direction of the house, he asked, 'Has Mr. Worthing returned from London yet? I was hoping for a word with him.'

'We do not expect him until Monday afternoon,' Miss Prism replied, at which Dr. Chasuble nodded. 'Ah, yes,' he said, 'I should have remembered. He usually likes to spend his Sundays in London. He is not one of those whose sole aim is enjoyment, as, by all accounts, that unfortunate young man his brother seems to be.' He stood for a moment in sad contemplation of Ernest Worthing's character, and then returned his thoughts to the present. 'But I must not disturb Egeria and her pupil any longer,' he said with a gallant bow.

'Egeria?' echoed Miss Prism, puzzled. 'My name is Lætitia, Doctor.'

Dr. Chasuble bowed again. 'A classical allusion, merely,' he said, 'drawn from the Pagan authors.' He turned to go, and as he did so asked, 'Shall I see both you ladies at Evensong?'

Realizing that the clergyman was about to leave, Miss Prism now decided that she would like to enjoy his company for a little longer. 'I think, dear Doctor, I *will* have a stroll with you,' she said. 'I find I have a headache after all, and a walk might do it good.'

Dr. Chasuble looked delighted. 'With pleasure, Miss

Prism, with pleasure,' he assured her. 'We might go as far as the school and back.'

'That would be delightful,' Miss Prism positively simpered. Then, addressing her pupil in a firm voice, she said, 'Cecily, you will read your Political Economy in my absence. The chapter on the Fall of the Rupee you may omit. It is somewhat too sensational. Even these metallic problems have their melodramatic side.'

Miss Prism took the Rector's proffered arm, and they set off down the path towards the garden gate. Once they were out of earshot, Cecily picked up several of the books from the table, and flung them down again. 'Horrid Political Economy,' she said crossly. 'Horrid Geography. Horrid, horrid German!'

Pouting, she was about to return to her diary when Merriman, her guardian's butler, approached from the house, bearing a salver on which was a card. 'Mr. Ernest Worthing has just driven over from the station, Miss Cecily,' he informed her. As Cecily took up the card, the tall, silver-haired butler added loftily, 'He has brought his luggage with him.'

' "Mr. Ernest Worthing, B.4, The Albany, London W.",' Cecily read aloud. 'Heavens!' she exclaimed. 'It's Uncle Jack's brother.' Looking up at the butler, she asked, 'Did you tell him that Mr. Worthing is still in town?'

'Yes, miss,' Merriman replied. 'He seemed very much disappointed. I mentioned that you and Miss Prism were in the garden, and he said he was most anxious to speak to you privately.'

Cecily gave the matter a moment's thought, then said, 'Ask Mr. Ernest Worthing to come out here. And I suppose you had better talk to the housekeeper about a room for him.'

'Yes, miss,' Merriman replied and returned to the house.

To herself, Cecily murmured pensively, 'I have never met any really wicked person before. I feel rather frightened. I am so afraid he will look just like everyone else.' She was about to confide this fear to her diary when Algernon Moncrieff emerged from the house, dressed as for an informal weekend in the country, and looking very gay and debonair. After a quick glance at him, Cecily thought, 'I was right. He does look like everyone else.'

Approaching her, Algernon politely raised his hat in greeting. 'You are my little cousin Cecily, I'm sure,' he said.

Cecily regarded him coolly. 'You are under some strange mistake,' she replied. 'I am not little. In fact, I believe I am more than usually tall for my age.'

Algernon seemed rather taken back by this response. He was about to speak when Cecily continued, 'But I am indeed your cousin Cecily. And you, I see from your card, are Uncle Jack's brother, my cousin Ernest.' Before he could reply, she added meaningfully, 'My wicked cousin Ernest.'

'Oh, I am not really wicked at all, Cousin Cecily,' Algernon protested. 'You mustn't think that I am wicked.'

This, however, was clearly not the right approach to

use with Cecily. 'If you are not,' she returned, 'then you have certainly been deceiving us in a very inexcusable manner.'

Algernon could think of no quick reply, and Cecily went on, 'I hope you have not been leading a double life, pretending to be wicked and being really good all the time. That would be hypocrisy.'

Algernon gazed at her in amazement. 'Oh!' he said, almost at a loss for words. Looking around for inspiration, he managed to blurt out, rather desperately, 'Well ... er, that is ... of course, I have been rather reckless.'

'I am glad to hear it,' answered Cecily.

'In fact,' Algernon continued, his confidence beginning to return, 'now that you mention the subject, I have been very bad in my own small way.'

Yet this too seemed to be not quite what Cecily wanted to hear, for her response was, 'I don't think you should be so proud of that.' Then, however, perhaps feeling that she was being unnecessarily censorious, she added graciously, 'Though I am sure it must have been very pleasant.'

'It is much pleasanter being here with you,' Algernon replied gallantly.

Cecily looked at him not altogether approvingly. 'I can't understand how you are here at all,' she said. 'Uncle Jack won't be back till Monday afternoon.'

His face a study in gravity, Algernon said, 'That is a great disappointment to me. I am obliged to go up to town by the first train on Monday morning. I have a business appointment that I am anxious ... to miss.'

'Couldn't you miss it anywhere else?'

'I'm afraid not. You see, the appointment is in London.'

'Well,' Cecily replied, 'I know, of course, how important it is not to keep a business engagement, if one wants to retain any sense of the beauty of life, but still I think you had better wait till Uncle Jack arrives. I know he wants to speak to you about your emigrating.'

Algernon was startled. 'About my what?' he asked.

'Your emigrating,' Cecily repeated. 'He has gone up to town to buy your outfit.'

'I certainly wouldn't let Jack buy my outfit,' Algernon exclaimed in horror. 'He has no taste in neckties at all.'

'I don't think you will require neckties,' Cecily reassured him. 'Uncle Jack is sending you to Australia.'

Algernon looked appalled. 'Australia! I'd sooner die,' he vowed.

'I distinctly remember,' said Cecily, 'Uncle Jack saying at dinner on Wednesday evening that you would have to choose between this world, the next world, and Australia.'

'Well,' Algernon declared, 'the accounts I have received of Australia and the next world are not particularly encouraging. This world is good enough for me, Cousin Cecily.'

'Yes, but are you good enough for it?' asked Cecily.

'I'm afraid I'm not that,' he admitted. 'That is why I want you to reform me. You might make that your mission, if you don't mind, Cousin Cecily.'

She considered for a moment, then replied, 'I'm afraid I've no time this afternoon.'

Algernon looked rueful. 'Well, would you mind my reforming *myself* this afternoon?' he asked.

'It is rather quixotic of you,' Cecily replied. 'But I think you should try.'

Algernon smiled. 'I will,' he said. 'I feel better already.'

Cecily studied him intently. 'You are looking a little worse,' she observed.

'That is because I am hungry,' he explained quickly.

She was immediately apologetic. 'How thoughtless of me,' she cried. 'I should have remembered that when one is going to lead an entirely new life, one requires regular and wholesome meals.' She rose from the table. 'Won't you come in?' she asked, gesturing towards the house.

'Thank you,' said Algernon. 'But may I have a buttonhole first? I never have any appetite unless I have a buttonhole first.'

Cecily looked around at the garden. Then, picking up a pair of scissors from the table, she went across to an exotic-looking shrub and enquired, 'Will a Maréchal Niel do?'

'Well, I'd rather have a *pink* rose.'

'Really? Why?' Cecily asked, as she stooped to cut a pink bud.

'Because you are like a pink rose, Cousin Cecily,' Algernon said, a sudden ardour in his voice.

Cecily regarded him thoughtfully. 'I don't think it can be right for you to talk to me like that. Miss Prism never says such things to me.'

'Then Miss Prism is a short-sighted old lady,' Algernon declared, as Cecily put the flower in his buttonhole. 'You are the prettiest girl I ever saw.'

'Miss Prism,' she returned primly, 'says that all good looks are a snare.'

'They are a snare,' Algernon agreed. 'But a snare that every sensible man would like to be caught in.'

'Oh, I don't think I would care to catch a sensible man,' answered Cecily. 'I shouldn't know what to talk to him about.' With that she led him indoors.

CHAPTER
SEVEN

CHAPTER SEVEN

A FEW minutes after Algernon and Cecily had gone into the house, Miss Prism and Dr. Chasuble returned from their walk and approached the table at which the governess and her pupil had been studying. Dr. Chasuble had, it seems, been resisting hints from Miss Prism that he needed a woman to look after him. 'But you are too much alone, dear Dr. Chasuble,' she insisted. 'You really should get married, you know. A misanthrope I can understand, but a womanthrope—never!'

With a scholar's shudder, the Rector replied, 'Believe me, Miss Prism, I do not deserve so neologistic a phrase. It is simply that the precept as well as the practice of the Primitive Church was distinctly against matrimony.'

'That,' Miss Prism observed sententiously, 'is obviously the reason why the Primitive Church has not lasted up to the present day.' She settled herself in her chair at the table, and looked up at him coyly. 'You do not seem to realize, dear Doctor, that, by persistently remaining single, you convert yourself into a permanent public temptation.' She emphasized this with a decisive nod. 'Men such as you,' she continued, 'should be more careful. This very celibacy can lead weaker vessels astray.'

Dr. Chasuble looked as though he did not understand. 'But is a man not equally attractive when he is married?' he asked, hesitantly.

Miss Prism appeared both surprised and shocked. 'No married man,' she said firmly, 'is ever attractive, except of course to his wife.'

The Rector bravely hazarded an attempt at humour. 'And often, I've been told, not even to his wife,' he remarked, with a laugh that was akin to a neigh.

This witticism was lost on Miss Prism, who responded with perfect seriousness, if not solemnity. 'That depends on the intellectual sympathies of the woman,' she explained. 'Maturity can always be depended upon.' She glanced up to see how he had received this *aperçu*. Noting an impassive countenance, she rephrased her observation. 'Ripeness can be trusted,' she offered, but still the Rector did not react. Miss Prism tried again. 'Young women are green,' she declared more bluntly.

Dr. Chasuble gave a start at this, and the governess hastened to explain. 'I spoke horticulturally,' she told him. 'My metaphor was drawn from fruits.' He smiled and nodded absently, at which Miss Prism decided that it might be more prudent to postpone any further discussion of the male psyche and its requirements. Looking around, she asked, 'But where is Cecily?'

Dr. Chasuble, too, looked about him. 'Perhaps she followed us up to the school?' he ventured.

Miss Prism was about to reply when her attention was diverted by an extraordinary sight. Her employer, Jack Worthing—to give him his country name—had entered the garden by an outside gate, and was walking slowly towards them. He was dressed in the deepest mourning, even down to black gloves and a crape band round his hat.

'Mr. Worthing!' Miss Prism exclaimed in astonishment.

'Mr. Worthing?' Canon Chasuble echoed, as though he could not believe his eyes.

'This is indeed a surprise, Mr. Worthing,' Miss Prism said as she went forward to greet him. 'We were not expecting you until Monday afternoon.'

Jack took Miss Prism's outstretched hand, and shook it in a tragic manner. 'I have returned sooner than I expected,' he announced gravely. Turning to the Rector, he greeted him with equal solemnity. 'Dr. Chasuble, I hope you are well?'

The cleric gazed at him enquiringly. 'Dear Mr Worthing,' he said, as he took Jack's hand, 'I trust this garb of woe does not betoken some terrible calamity?'

Jack bowed his head. 'My brother,' he murmured.

Miss Prism, her expression serious, asked, 'More shameful debts and extravagance?'

'Still leading his life of pleasure?' Canon Chasuble surmised.

Jack shook his head. 'Dead.'

Dr. Chasuble looked shocked. 'Your brother Ernest is dead?' he asked.

'Quite dead,' Jack replied.

Miss Prism's face was stern as she spoke. 'What a lesson for him!' she exclaimed. 'I trust he will profit by it.'

Dr. Chasuble's attempt to comfort the bereaved Jack was at least more conventional, if not much less censorious. 'Mr. Worthing,' he intoned, as though from the pulpit, 'I offer you my sincere condolences.' He paused for reflection, before continuing, 'You have at least the consolation of knowing that you were always the most generous and forgiving of brothers.'

Jack shook his head sadly. 'Poor Ernest,' he sighed. 'He had many faults, but it is a sad, sad blow.'

'Very sad indeed,' Dr. Chasuble agreed. 'Were you with him at the end?'

'No,' the other replied. 'He died abroad. In Paris, as a matter of fact. I had a telegram last night from the manager of the Grand Hotel.'

'Was the cause of death mentioned?' the Rector asked.

'A severe chill, it seems.'

Miss Prism nodded sagely. 'As a man sows,' she observed, 'so shall he reap.'

Dr. Chasuble raised a hand. 'Charity, dear Miss Prism, charity,' he admonished her. 'None of us are perfect.' After a moment's thought he continued, 'I myself am peculiarly susceptible to draughts.' Turning again to Jack, he enquired, 'Will the interment take place here?'

'No,' Jack replied. 'He seems to have expressed a desire to be buried in Paris.'

'In Paris!' Dr. Chasuble exclaimed, shocked. 'I fear that hardly points to any very serious state of mind at the last.' He shook his head despairingly, and then, as the thought suddenly occurred to him, added, 'You would no doubt wish me to make some slight allusion to this tragic domestic affliction in church next Sunday.'

As though so overcome with emotion as to be unable to speak, Jack pressed the Rector's hand convulsively. 'My sermon on the meaning of the manna in the wilderness,' that gentleman went on, 'can be adapted to almost any occasion, joyful, or, as in the present case, distressing.'

A sigh arose from all three of them. After a pause, Dr. Chasuble continued, 'I have preached it at harvest celebrations, christenings, confirmations, on days of humiliation, and festal days. The last time I delivered it was in the Cathedral, as a charity sermon on behalf of the Society for the Prevention of Discontent among the Upper Orders.' Since his listeners seemed a trifle bemused by this information, Dr. Chasuble sought to reassure them. 'The Bishop, who was present,' he said, 'was much struck by some of the analogies I drew'.

Jack's expression of grief had changed somewhat during the clergyman's recital. 'Ah, that reminds me,' he remarked, 'You mentioned christenings, I think, Dr. Chasuble? I suppose you know how to christen all right?'

Seeing the sudden look of offence on Dr. Chasuble's face, Jack hastened to soften his words. 'I mean, of course,' he stammered, 'that you are continually christening, aren't you?'

'It is, I regret to say,' Miss Prism intervened disapprovingly, 'one of the Rector's most constant duties in this parish. I have often spoken to the poorer classes on the subject. But they don't seem to know what thrift is.'

Wisely choosing to ignore this uncalled-for condemnation, Dr. Chasuble asked, 'But is there any particular infant in whom you are interested, Mr. Worthing? Your brother, I believe, was unmarried, was he not?'

'Oh yes,' Jack replied, abstractedly.

'People who live entirely for pleasure usually are unmarried,' Miss Prism observed bitterly.

'It is not for any child, dear Doctor, though of course I am very fond of children,' Jack told the Rector. 'No, the fact is, I would like to be christened myself.' His words were greeted with a look of incomprehension, but he continued, 'This afternoon, in fact, if you have nothing better to do.'

Dr. Chasuble, taken entirely by surprise, expostulated, 'But surely, Mr. Worthing, you have been christened already?'

Jack looked him in the eye, and replied firmly, 'I can't be sure of that. I certainly don't remember anything about it.'

'But have you any grave doubts on the subject?' the clergyman persisted.

'I certainly intend to have,' Jack replied. 'Of course, I don't know if the thing would bother you in any way, or if you think I am a little too old now.'

'Not at all,' the Rector replied. 'The sprinkling and, indeed, the immersion of adults is a perfectly canonical practice.'

'Immersion!' Jack exclaimed in alarm.

'You need have no apprehension,' Dr. Chasuble assured him. 'Sprinkling is all that is necessary, or indeed, I think, advisable. After all, our weather is so changeable.' He suddenly, and rather unnervingly, beamed at Jack, and asked, 'At what hour would you wish the ceremony performed?'

After a moment's thought Jack replied airily, 'Oh, I might trot around at about five, if that would suit you.'

'Perfectly, perfectly. In fact I have two similar ceremonies to perform at that time. A case of twins that occurred recently in one of the outlying cottages on your own estate. Poor Jenkins the carter, a most hard-working man.'

Jack frowned. 'Oh,' he sighed, 'I don't see much fun in being christened along with other babies. It would be childish.' He consulted his pocket diary, and then asked, 'Would half-past five do?'

'Admirably! admirably!' said Canon Chasuble. He took out his pocket-watch and glanced at it. 'And now, dear Mr. Worthing, I will not intrude any longer into a house of sorrow. I would merely beg you not to be too much bowed down by grief. What seem to us to be bitter trials are often blessings in disguise.'

'This,' Miss Prism observed tartly, 'seems to me a blessing of an extremely obvious kind.'

At that moment, Cecily emerged from the house. 'Uncle Jack!' she cried. 'Oh, I am so pleased to see you back.' Her eyes fell on his attire, and she exclaimed, 'But what horrid clothes you have got on. Do go and change them.'

'*Cecily!*' Miss Prism, shocked by her pupil's insensitive behaviour, took refuge in reprimand.

'My child, my child,' the Rector, too, admonished her. But Cecily had already advanced upon her Uncle Jack, who responded by kissing her brow in a melancholy manner.

'What is the matter, Uncle Jack?' the girl asked. 'Do try to look happy. You look as if you had toothache, and I have got such a lovely surprise for you. Who do you think is in the dining-room?'

Since Jack merely raised his eyebrows enquiringly, she declared triumphantly, 'Your brother!'

Jack looked blank. 'Who?' he asked, weakly.

'Your brother Ernest,' said Cecily. 'He arrived about half an hour ago.'

'What nonsense,' Jack retorted incautiously. 'I haven't got a brother.'

'Oh, don't say that,' Cecily pleaded. 'However badly he may have behaved to you in the past, he is still your brother. You couldn't be so heartless as to disown him.'

As Jack looked about him in confusion, she continued, 'I'll tell him to come out. And you will shake hands with him, won't you, Uncle Jack?' Without waiting for an answer, she ran back into the house.

Canon Chasuble clapped his hands happily, turning a radiant smile upon Jack Worthing and Miss Prism. 'These are very joyful tidings indeed, are they not?' he asked.

Miss Prism was not so certain. 'After we had all been resigned to his loss,' she remarked, 'his sudden return seems to me to be peculiarly distressing.'

Jack's mind was whirling. 'My brother is in the dining-room?' he murmured to himself incredulously. To the others, he merely said, 'I don't know what this all means. I think it is perfectly absurd.'

All three of them turned towards the house, and observed Algernon and Cecily, hand in hand, coming out into the garden. The pair slowly made their way to Jack, who exclaimed involuntarily, 'Good heavens!' and motioned his friend away.

Algernon, however, stood his ground. 'Brother John,' he declared, 'I have come down from town to tell you that I am very sorry for all the trouble I have given you, and that I intend to lead a better life in the future.' He held his hand out to Jack, who glared at him and declined to take it.

Cecily gave her uncle a look of strong disapproval. 'Uncle Jack,' she protested, 'surely you are not going to refuse your own brother's hand?'

With a furious look at Algernon, Jack replied, 'Nothing will induce me to take his hand. I think his coming down here is absolutely disgraceful. He knows perfectly well why.'

'Uncle Jack, do be nice,' Cecily pleaded. 'There is some good in everyone. Ernest'—and here she glanced admiringly at Algernon—'has just been telling me about his poor invalid friend Mr. Bunbury whom he goes to visit so often. And surely there must be a great deal of good in someone who is kind to an invalid, and leaves the pleasures of London to sit by a bed of pain.'

'Oh, he has been talking about Bunbury, has he?' Jack growled.

'Yes,' replied Cecily. 'He has told me all about poor Mr. Bunbury, and his terrible state of health.'

'Bunbury!' Jack exploded. 'Well, I won't have him talk to you about Bunbury or about anything else. It is enough to drive one perfectly frantic.'

Algernon assumed a hurt expression. 'Of course it's true that the faults were all on my side,' he admitted. 'But I must say that I find Brother John's coldness to me peculiarly painful. I expected a more enthusiastic welcome, especially considering that this is the first time I have come here.'

'Uncle Jack,' said Cecily, 'if you don't shake hands with your brother Ernest, I shall never forgive you.'

'Never forgive me?'

'Never, never, never!' Cecily shouted, her anger driving her almost to tears.

Jack looked around at Canon Chasuble and Miss Prism, who both stood with expectant expressions on their faces. After a pause, he managed a dignified utterance. 'Very well,' he conceded. 'But this is the last time I shall ever do it.' Still glaring at Algernon, he shook hands with him, and immediately turned away.

'It is pleasant, is it not,' Canon Chasuble observed, 'to see so perfect a reconciliation?' Then, addressing the ladies, he suggested, 'I think we might leave the two brothers together.'

Miss Prism nodded agreement. 'Cecily, you will come with us,' she ordered.

'Certainly, Miss Prism,' Cecily replied. 'My little task of reconciliation is over.'

'You have performed a beautiful action today, dear child,' said Canon Chasuble.

'We must not be premature in our judgments,' Miss Prism remarked somewhat obscurely as the three of them went off together, Cecily walking jauntily beside the two older people with a cry of 'Oh, I feel so very happy.'

CHAPTER
EIGHT

CHAPTER EIGHT

WHEN Cecily, Miss Prism and Canon Chasuble had disappeared around the side of the house, Jack turned angrily to Algernon, who stood looking after them with an expression of smug satisfaction on his face. 'You young scoundrel, Algy,' he declared, 'you must get out of this place as soon as possible. I don't allow any Bunburying here.'

Algernon was about to reply when his attention was diverted by the sight of the butler, Merriman, who, emerging from the house, hastened across the lawn towards them. Addressing his employer, Merriman said, 'I have put Mr. Ernest's things in the room next to yours, sir. I assume that is all right?'

'What?' Jack exclaimed, directing a look of utter consternation at the butler.

'Mr. Ernest's luggage, sir,' Merriman explained patiently. 'I have unpacked it and put it in the room next to your own.'

'His luggage?'

'Yes, sir,' Merriman replied. 'Three portmanteaus, a

dressing-case, two hat-boxes, and a large luncheon-basket.'

'I am afraid I can't stay more than a week this time,' Algernon explained, fearing that his luggage was thought to be inadequate.

Ignoring him, Jack said, 'Merriman, order the dog-cart at once. Mr. Ernest has been suddenly called back to town.'

Merriman uttered an imperturbable 'Yes, sir,' and went back into the house.

'What a fearful liar you are, Jack,' Algernon said cheerfully. 'I have not been called back to town at all.'

'Oh, yes you have,' Jack muttered between clenched teeth.

'Well, I haven't heard anyone call me.'

Jack gave him a fierce look. 'Your duty as a gentleman calls you back.'

'My duty as a gentleman,' Algernon observed, 'has never interfered with my pleasures in the smallest degree.'

'I can quite understand that,' Jack snarled.

For Algernon, however, the situation had been satisfactorily resolved. Rubbing his hands in glee, he exclaimed, 'I must say, Cecily is an absolute darling.'

'You are not to talk of Miss Cardew like that,' Jack snapped. 'I don't like it.'

'Well, I don't like your clothes,' Algernon retorted. 'You look positively ridiculous in them. Why on earth don't you go up and change?'

'I am in mourning for my brother,' Jack muttered.

Algernon gave a snort of derision. 'It is perfectly

THE IMPORTANCE OF BEING EARNEST

childish to be in mourning—in deep mourning, I observe—for a man who is actually staying for a whole week with you in your house as a guest. Indeed, I call it grotesque.'

Coming up close to Algernon, Jack fixed him with a furious eye. 'You are certainly not staying with me for a whole week, as a guest or anything else,' he declared. 'You have got to leave. I suggest the four-fifteen train.'

Algernon shook his head, his expression smugly serene. 'I certainly won't leave you while you are in mourning. It would be most unfriendly. If I were in mourning, I'm sure you would stay with me. I should think it very unkind if you didn't.'

Jack looked desperate. 'Well, will you go if I change my clothes?' he asked.

After a moment's thought, Algernon replied, 'Yes, if you are not too long. I never saw anybody take so long to dress—and with such little result.'

'Well, at any rate,' Jack replied, 'that is better than being always over-dressed as you are.'

'If I am occasionally a little over-dressed,' Algernon said, 'I make up for it by being always immensely over-educated.'

Jack was by now exasperated. 'Your vanity is ridiculous, your conduct an outrage, and your presence in my garden utterly absurd,' he shouted. Then, lowering his voice a trifle, he continued, 'However, you have got to catch the four-fifteen, and I hope you will have a pleasant journey back to town. I'm afraid this Bunburying, as you call it, has not been a great success for you,' he added, with a superior smile. Turning abruptly, he strode off to the house.

'I think it has been a great success,' Algernon called after him. 'I'm in love with Cecily, and that is everything.'

If his friend heard him, he chose not to reply, but entered the house, slamming the door behind him.

At that moment, Cecily reappeared from a secluded corner of the garden, once more with a watering-can in her hand. Slowly she approached Algernon, stopping from time to time to water the flowers. 'I must talk to her before I go,' he thought to himself, 'and make arrangements for another Bunbury.' He raised his hat as Cecily came up to him.

'Oh, I merely came back to water the roses,' Cecily explained. 'I thought you would be with Uncle Jack.'

'He's gone to order the dog-cart for me,' he said ruefully.

'Oh? Is he going to take you for a nice drive?'

'Alas, no,' Algernon replied. 'I'm afraid he's going to send me away.'

Cecily looked more than a little upset to hear this. 'Does that mean we have got to part?' she asked.

'I am afraid so,' sighed Algernon. 'It's a very painful parting.'

'It is always painful to part from people whom one has known for a very brief space of time,' Cecily confessed. 'The absence of old friends one can endure with equanimity. But even a momentary separation from anyone to whom one has just been introduced is almost unbearable.'

'Thank you,' was Algernon's heart-felt response. He was about to say more when he caught sight of Merriman approaching from the house.

'The dog-cart is at the door, sir,' the butler announced.

Algernon turned appealingly to Cecily, who quickly came to his rescue. 'The dog-cart can wait, Merriman,' she said, 'for five minutes.'

'Yes, miss,' Merriman replied, and returned to the house.

Algernon watched him go, and then turned to Cecily, his gaze one of complete adoration. 'I hope, Cecily,' he declared solemnly, 'that I shall not offend you if I state quite frankly and openly that you seem to me to be in every way the visible personification of absolute perfection.'

'I think your frankness does you great credit, Ernest,' she assured him with a smile of great sweetness 'If you will allow me, I shall copy your remarks into my diary.' She went over to the table, opened her diary and began to write in it.

'Do you really keep a diary?' Ernest asked. 'I'd give anything to look at it.' He assumed a child-like, pleading expression. 'May I?'

'Oh, no,' Cecily replied, quickly putting her hand over the book. 'You see, it is simply a very young girl's record of her own thoughts and impressions, and consequently meant for publication. When it appears in volume form, I hope you will order a copy.' Seeing the look of disappointment on Algernon's face, she added quickly, 'But, please, my dear Ernest, don't stop. I delight in taking down from dictation. I have got as far as "absolute perfection". You may go on. I am quite ready for more.'

Somewhat taken aback, he gave a nervous cough.

'Oh, don't cough, Ernest,' said Cecily. 'When one is dictating, one should speak fluently, and not cough. Besides, I don't know how to spell a cough.'

Algernon took a deep breath and began to speak very rapidly. 'Cecily, ever since I first looked upon your wonderful and incomparable beauty,' he gabbled, 'I have dared to love you wildly, passionately, devotedly, hopelessly.'

Stopping him with a wave of her hand, Cecily remarked, 'I don't think you should tell me that you love me wildly, passionately, devotedly, hopelessly.' When he looked at her enquiringly, she explained, '"Hopelessly" doesn't seem to make much sense, does it?'

Closing his eyes, Algernon breathed rapturously. 'Cecily,' he murmured. He opened his eyes quickly when he heard the voice of Merriman, who had approached them unobserved. 'The dog-cart is waiting, sir,' the butler announced.

'Tell it to come round next week at the same hour,' ordered Algernon.

Merriman looked at Cecily for confirmation, but when she made no sign, her gaze and her attention firmly centred upon Algernon, the butler replied, 'Yes, sir,' and retired once more to the house.

When he had gone, Cecily rose from the table and

came up close to Algernon. Gazing into his eyes, she whispered, 'Uncle Jack would be very much annoyed if he knew you were staying on till next week at the same hour.'

'Oh, I don't care about Jack,' cried Algernon. 'I don't care about anybody in the world but you. I love you, Cecily.' Then, suddenly struck by a thought, he added anxiously, 'You will marry me, won't you?'

A peal of laughter greeted his words. 'You silly boy! Of course! Why, we have been engaged for the last four months.'

'Engaged?' he asked, startled. 'For the last four months?'

Cecily consulted her diary, turning over several pages. 'Yes,' she confirmed, 'it will be exactly four months next Thursday.'

Confusion was written plain on Algernon's face. 'But how did we become engaged?' he asked.

'Well,' Cecily replied, adopting a confidential tone, 'ever since dear Uncle Jack first confessed to us that he had a younger brother who was very wicked and bad, you of course have formed the chief topic of conversation between myself and my governess, Miss Prism. And, as I'm sure you know, a man who is much talked about is always very attractive. One feels there must be something in him, after all.' Gazing at Algernon tenderly, she admitted, 'I daresay it was foolish of me, but I fell in love with you, Ernest.'

'Darling!' Algernon exclaimed joyfully. Then, anxious to learn more, he asked, 'But when was the engagement actually settled?'

Cecily consulted her diary again. 'On the fourteenth of February last. Worn out by your entire ignorance of my existence, I determined to end the matter one way or the other, and after a long struggle with myself I accepted you.' She looked around, and then pointed to a distant part of the garden. 'It happened under that dear old tree over there.' Holding her left hand up to Algernon's face, she continued, 'The next day I bought this little ring in your name, and this'— she exhibited her wrist—'this is the little bangle with the true lover's knot that I promised you I would always wear.'

'Did I give you this?' Algernon asked, examining it. 'It's very pretty, isn't it?'

'Yes, you have wonderfully good taste, Ernest. It's the excuse I've always given for your leading such a bad life.' She knelt down by the side of the table, opened a box, and produced a bundle of letters tied up with blue ribbon. 'And this,' she revealed, 'is the box in which I keep all your dear letters.'

'My letters?' Algernon wondered. 'But ... my own sweet Cecily, I have never written you any letters.'

'You need hardly remind me of that, Ernest,' she replied, rather sharply. 'I remember only too well that I was forced to write your letters for you. I wrote always three times a week, and occasionally more often.'

Algernon was entranced. 'Oh, do let me read them, Cecily,' he urged.

'I couldn't possibly do that,' she answered. 'They would make you far too conceited.' Replacing the letters in the box, she smiled happily as she recalled their contents. 'The three you wrote me after I had broken off the engagement,' she confided, 'are so beautiful, and so badly spelt, that even now I can hardly read them without crying a little.'

Algernon seemed extremely upset by this. 'Do you mean to say that our engagement was broken off?'

'Of course it was,' Cecily replied. 'On the twenty-second of March. You can see the entry if you like.' Finding the appropriate page, she showed it to him as she read out the entry. '"Today I broke off my engagement to Ernest. I feel it is better to do so. The weather still continues charming."'

'But why on earth did you break it off?' Algernon asked. 'What had I done? I had done nothing at all.' He shook his head reproachfully. 'Cecily, I am very much hurt indeed to hear that you broke it off. Particularly when the weather was so charming.'

'It would hardly have been a really serious engagement if it hadn't been broken off at least once,' she assured him. 'But I forgave you before the week was out.'

Algernon gave a sigh of relief, and knelt before her. 'What a perfect angel you are, Cecily,' he said.

Looking down at him, Cecily smiled tenderly. 'You dear romantic boy,' she breathed. He grasped her hand, kissing it ardently, and she ran her fingers through his hair. 'I hope your hair curls naturally, my dearest. Does it?' she asked, stooping to examine it.

'Yes, of course, darling, with a little help from others,' Algernon assured her.

'I am so glad,' Cecily murmured.

Still on his knees, Algernon gazed up at her. 'Promise me that you'll never break off our engagement again, Cecily,' he begged her.

'I don't think I could possibly break it off now that I have actually met you,' she admitted. 'Besides, of course, there is the question of your name.'

'My name?' Algernon asked, nervously.

Cecily smiled tenderly down at him. 'You must not laugh at me, darling, but it had always been a girlish dream of mine to love someone whose name was Ernest.'

Startled, Algernon rose to his feet.

'There is something in that name,' Cecily continued, 'that seems to inspire absolute confidence. I pity any poor married woman whose husband is not called Ernest.'

Algernon regarded her with dismay. 'But, my dear child, do you mean to say you could not love me if I had some other name?'

'What other name?' Cecily asked.

Algernon looked about in desperation. 'Oh, any name you like. What about . . . Algernon, for instance?'

Cecily pouted. 'But I don't like the name of Algernon.'

'Well, my own dear, sweet, loving little darling,' Algernon burbled, 'I really can't see why you should object to the name of Algernon. It is not at all a bad name. In fact, it is a rather aristocratic name. Half of the chaps who get into the Bankruptcy Court are called Algernon.'

When Cecily made no response to this, he moved

closer to her and continued, 'But seriously, Cecily, if my name was Algy, couldn't you love me?'

Without hesitation, Cecily shook her head. 'I might respect you, Ernest,' she said, 'I might admire your character. But I fear that I should not be able to give you my undivided attention.'

'Oh dear.' Picking up his hat from the table, he addressed his betrothed urgently. 'Cecily, your Rector here is, I suppose, thoroughly experienced in the practice of all the rites and ceremonials of the Church?'

'Oh, yes,' she assured him. 'Dr. Chasuble is a most learned man. He has never written a single book, so you can imagine how much he must know.'

Algernon smiled distractedly. 'I must see him at once on a most important christening—I mean, on most important business.'

'Oh!' Cecily exclaimed in surprise.

'I shan't be away more than half an hour,' he promised.

Cecily gave him a stern look. 'Considering that we have been engaged since February the fourteenth, and that I only met you today for the first time,' she replied, 'I think it is rather hard that you should leave me for so long a period as half an hour. Couldn't you make it twenty minutes?'

Algernon uttered an exclamation that was half a growl of impatience and half a cry of delight. 'I'll be back in no time,' he said. He kissed her quickly and rushed off down the garden.

Cecily watched his retreating figure until it was out of sight. 'What an impetuous boy he is,' she sighed. 'I do like his hair so much.' Her face lit up as she suddenly remembered a crucial task she had to perform. 'I must enter his proposal in my diary right away,' she told herself. She returned to the table, opened the diary and began to write.

CHAPTER NINE

CHAPTER NINE

CECILY was still writing excitedly in her diary several minutes later when Merriman appeared again. Coughing to engage her attention, he waited for her to finish a sentence. When she looked up, he announced, 'A Miss Fairfax has just called to see Mr. Worthing, miss. On very important business, Miss Fairfax states.'

Cecily looked surprised. 'Isn't Mr. Worthing in his library?' she asked.

'No, miss. Mr. Worthing went out in the direction of the Rectory some time ago.'

After a moment's thought, Cecily told him to show the lady out into the garden. 'Mr. Worthing is sure to be back soon,' she added. 'Meanwhile, you can bring tea to us out here.'

'Yes, miss,' Merriman replied, and went to do her bidding.

'Who can Miss Fairfax be?' Cecily wondered. 'Perhaps she is one of the good elderly women who are associated with Uncle Jack in some of his philanthropic work in London.' She wrinkled her nose. 'I don't quite like women who are interested in philanthropic work. I think it is so forward of them.'

Just then Merriman came back from the house, now with Gwendolen Fairfax. 'Miss Fairfax,' he announced, and returned indoors.

Cecily advanced to meet the visitor. 'Pray let me introduce myself to you,' she said, sweetly. 'My name is Cecily Cardew.'

'Cecily Cardew?' Gwendolen echoed, shaking hands. 'What a very sweet name! Something tells me that we are going to be great friends. I like you already more than I can say.' She smiled graciously. 'My first impressions of people are never wrong.'

Returning her smile, Cecily replied, 'How nice of you to like me so much after we have known each other such a comparatively short time.' She gestured Gwendolen to a chair. 'Pray sit down.'

Gwendolen hesitated. 'I may call you Cecily, may I not?' she asked.

'With pleasure!' Cecily replied.

'And you will always call me Gwendolen, won't you?'

'If you wish,' Cecily responded.

Gwendolen looked satisfied. 'Then that is all quite settled, is it not?' she asked.

'I hope so,' said Cecily.

They looked each other over admiringly and, after a pause, both sat down.

Gwendolen, having glanced around at the garden, turned to Cecily. 'Perhaps this might be a favourable opportunity for me to mention who I am,' she remarked. 'My father is Lord Bracknell.' When Cecily said nothing, she continued, 'You have never heard of Papa, I suppose?'

Cecily thought for a moment and then shook her head. 'I don't think so.'

Nodding in understanding, Gwendolen continued, 'Papa, I am glad to say, is entirely unknown outside the family circle. I think that is quite as it should be.' Drawing back her shoulders, and again momentarily surveying the landscape, she continued, 'The home seems to me to be the proper sphere for the man.' It might have been her mother speaking, for Gwendolen echoed not only the matter but also the manner of Lady Bracknell's utterance. 'And certainly, once a man begins to neglect his domestic duties, he becomes painfully effeminate, does he not? And I don't like men to be effeminate. It makes them so very attractive.' She paused. Then, gazing directly at Cecily, she declared, 'My mamma, Cecily, has remarkably strict views on education, and she has brought me up to be extremely short-sighted. It is part of her system. Do you mind my looking at you through my glasses?'

'Oh, not at all, Gwendolen,' said Cecily. 'I am very fond of being looked at.'

Raising her lorgnette to her eyes, Gwendolen examined Cecily very carefully. Then she observed, 'You are here on a short visit, I suppose.'

'Oh, no! I live here,' returned Cecily.

'Really?' Gwendolen's tone was severe. Looking the other girl up and down, she ventured to surmise, 'Your mother, no doubt, or some female relative of advanced years, resides here also?'

'Oh, no! I have no mother, nor, in fact, any relations,' Cecily explained.

'Indeed?' Gwendolen sounded none too happy to hear this.

'You see,' Cecily continued, 'My dear guardian, with the assistance of Miss Prism, has the arduous task of looking after me.'

'Your guardian?' Gwendolen prompted, suspicion lurking in her voice.

'Yes, my guardian,' Cecily repeated innocently. 'I am Mr. Worthing's ward.'

'Oh. It is strange he never mentioned to me that he had a ward. How secretive of him. He grows more interesting hourly,' Gwendolen observed. 'I am not sure, however, that the news inspires me with feelings of unmixed delight.' She rose, and walked around the table, almost menacingly, to Cecily. 'I am very fond of you, Cecily,' she affirmed. 'I have liked you ever since I met you. But I am bound to state that, now that I know you are Mr. Worthing's ward, I cannot help expressing a wish that you were . . .' She made an impatient gesture, and then resumed. 'A wish that you were . . . well, just a little older than you seem to be—and not quite so very alluring in appearance. In fact, if I may speak candidly . . .' She paused again.

'Pray do,' Cecily urged her. 'I think that whenever one has anything unpleasant to say, one should always be quite candid.'

Gwendolen gave a haughty smile. 'Well, to speak with perfect candour, Cecily,' she declared, 'I wish that you were fully forty-two, and more than usually plain for your age. Ernest has a strong, upright nature. He is the very soul of truth and honour. Disloyalty would be as impossible to him as deception. But even men of the noblest possible moral character are extremely susceptible to the influence of the physical charms of others.'

Cecily made an attempt to interrupt, but, silencing her with an imperious gesture, Gwendolen continued, 'Modern, no less than Ancient History, supplies us with many extremely painful examples of what I refer to. If it were not so, indeed, history would be quite unreadable.'

She paused for breath, and Cecily took the opportunity to ask, 'I beg your pardon, Gwendolen, but did you say Ernest?'

'Yes,' replied Gwendolen, shortly.

'Oh, but it is not Mr. Ernest Worthing who is my guardian,' Cecily explained. 'It is his brother. His elder brother.'

Gwendolen sat down again abruptly, astonished. With a formidable glare at Cecily, she observed frostily, 'Ernest never mentioned to me that he had a brother.'

'I am very sorry to say they have not been on good terms for a long time,' Cecily told her.

'Ah! That accounts for it,' Gwendolen answered. 'And, now that I think of it, I have never heard any man mention his brother. The subject seems distasteful to most men.' Her smile returned, and she bestowed it upon Cecily. 'My dear, you have lifted a load from my mind. I was growing almost anxious. It would have been terrible if any cloud had come across a friendship like ours, would it not?'

The two young ladies smiled sweetly at each other, but Gwendolen felt it prudent to enquire, 'Of course, you are quite, quite certain that it is not Mr. Ernest Worthing who is your guardian?'

'Quite certain,' Cecily assured her. She paused, then added, 'In fact, I am going to be his.'

The smile left Gwendolen's face. 'I beg your pardon?'

Shyly and confidingly, Cecily murmured, 'Dearest Gwendolen, there is no reason why I should make a secret of it to you. Our little county newspaper is sure to chronicle the fact next week. Mr. Ernest Worthing and I are engaged to be married.'

Gwendolen rose. 'My darling Cecily,' she said, quite politely, 'I think there must be some slight error. Mr. Ernest Worthing is engaged to me. The announcement will appear in the *Morning Post* on Saturday at the latest.'

Cecily rose and addressed Gwendolen with equal politeness. 'I am afraid you must be under some misconception. Ernest proposed to me exactly ten minutes ago.' She picked up her diary, and pointed out the latest entry.

Gwendolen examined the diary very carefully through her lorgnette, then said, 'It is very curious, for he asked me to be his wife yesterday afternoon at five-thirty. If you would care to verify the incident, please do so.' Opening her purse, she produced a small book. 'I never travel without my diary. One should always have something sensational to read in the train.' She found the appropriate page, and held it out. 'I am so sorry, dear Cecily, if it is any disappointment to you,' she said sympathetically, 'but I am afraid *I* have the prior claim.'

Cecily glanced cursorily at the diary before remark-ing, 'It would distress me more than I can tell you, dear Gwendolen, if it caused you any mental or physical anguish, but I feel bound to point out that since Ernest proposed to you he clearly has changed his mind.'

'If the poor fellow has been entrapped into any foolish promise,' said Gwendolen meditatively, 'I shall consider it my duty to rescue him at once, and with a firm hand.'

Cecily sighed, 'Whatever unfortunate entanglement my dear boy may have got into, I will never reproach him with it after we are married.'

She had spoken thoughtfully, even sadly, but to little avail, for Gwendolen's face became a study in smoul-dering fury. 'Do you allude to me, Miss Cardew, as an *entanglement*? You are presumptuous. On an occasion of this kind, it becomes more than a moral duty to speak one's mind. It becomes a pleasure.'

'Do you suggest, Miss Fairfax,' retorted Cecily, 'that I entrapped Ernest into an engagement? How dare you? This is no time for wearing the shallow mask of manners. When I see a spade, I call it a spade.'

Gwendolen smiled. 'I am glad to say,' she said sarcas-tically, 'that I have never seen a spade. It is obvious that our social spheres have been widely different.'

Cecily was about to offer an appropriately acid reply when she noticed that Merriman was approaching from the house with a tray on which there were tea-pot and tea-cups; he was followed by a footman who carried a salver, a table-cloth and a plate-stand. The presence of the servants exercised a restraining influence, under which the young ladies chafed.

'Shall I lay tea here as usual, miss?' Merriman asked Cecily, who replied calmly but sternly, 'Yes, as usual.'

He began to clear the table and to lay the cloth, while Cecily and Gwendolen glared at each other.

At length, Gwendolen felt obliged to break the silence. 'Are there many interesting walks in the vicinity, Miss Cardew?' she asked.

'Oh, yes,' answered Cecily, 'a great many. From the top of one of the hills quite close to here, one can see five counties.'

'Five counties!' Gwendolen exclaimed. 'I don't think I should like that. I hate crowds.'

'I suppose that is why you live in town,' Cecily said, sweetly. At this, Gwendolen bit her lip and tapped her foot nervously with her parasol. Then, making an effort to pull herself together, she looked around and commented 'Quite a well-kept garden, this is, Miss Cardew.'

Cecily forced a wooden smile. 'So glad you like it, Miss Fairfax,' she replied coldly.

'I had no idea there were so many flowers in the country,' Gwendolen observed.

'Oh,' Cecily replied, 'flowers are as common here, Miss Fairfax, as people are in London.'

It was Gwendolen's turn to give a frigid smile. 'Personally,' she observed tartly, 'I cannot understand how anybody manages to exist in the country—if anybody who is anybody does.' She ostentatiously stifled a yawn. 'The country always bores me to death.'

'Ah,' said Cecily. 'This is what the newspapers call agricultural depression, is it not? I believe the aristocracy are suffering very much from it just at present. It is almost an epidemic amongst them, I have been told.' Gesturing towards the tea-pot and cups, she asked with studied politeness, 'May I offer you some tea, Miss Fairfax?'

With an equally elaborate politeness, Gwendolen replied, 'Thank you.' To herself she thought, 'Detestable girl! But I do require tea!'

'Sugar?' asked Cecily, in a voice that was all sweetness.

'No, thank you,' Gwendolen answered, superciliously. 'Sugar is not fashionable any more.'

With an angry look at her, Cecily took up the tongs and put four lumps of sugar into Gwendolen's cup. Then, with another sweet smile, she enquired, 'Cake, or bread and butter?'

Sounding bored, Gwendolen replied, 'Bread and butter, please. Cake is rarely seen at the best houses nowadays.'

Cecily calmly cut a very large slice of cake and put it on a plate. 'Hand that to Miss Fairfax,' she told Merriman. He imperturbably did her bidding, then went back into the house with the footman.

Gwendolen took a sip of her tea, grimaced, and put down the cup at once. Reaching out a hand for the bread and butter, she found that it was cake. She sat still for a moment in contemplation, and then rose indignantly. 'You have filled my tea with lumps of sugar,' she told Cecily, 'and, although I most distinctly

asked for bread and butter, you have given me cake.'
She made 'cake' sound as though it were poison. 'I am
known for the gentleness of my disposition, and the
extraordinary sweetness of my nature, but I warn you,
Miss Cardew, you may go too far.'

Cecily also rose. 'To save my poor, innocent, trusting
boy from the machinations of any other girl, there are
no lengths to which I would not go,' she declared.

They faced each other in cold belligerence.

'From the moment I saw you,' Gwendolen announced
in ringing tones, 'I distrusted you. I felt that you were
false and vicious. I am never deceived in such matters.
My first impressions of people are invariably correct.'

'It seems to me, Miss Fairfax,' Cecily observed icily,
her chin jutting in determination, 'that I am trespassing
on your valuable time. No doubt you have many other
calls of a similar character to make in the neighbour-
hood.'

The two young women stood glaring defiantly at
each other.

CHAPTER
TEN

CHAPTER TEN

GWENDOLEN looked as though she might strike Cecily, but her attention was diverted by the sight of Jack Worthing striding towards them across the lawn. 'Ernest!' she greeted him. 'My own Ernest.'

'Gwendolen! Darling!' Jack cried. He was about to embrace her, but she drew back.

'A moment!' she almost barked at him. Then, adjusting her voice to a more polite level, she asked, pointing to Cecily, 'Could you tell me if you are engaged to be married to this young lady?'

Jack laughed. 'To dear little Cecily? Of course not! What could have put such an idea into your pretty little head?'

'Thank you,' Gwendolen replied. She offered him her cheek. 'You may kiss me.'

In a voice of extreme sweetness, Cecily said, 'I knew there must be some misunderstanding, Miss Fairfax. The gentleman whose arm is at present around your waist is my guardian, Mr. John Worthing.'

'I beg your pardon?' said Gwendolen.

'This,' Cecily explained, 'is Uncle Jack.'

Gwendolen recoiled. '*Jack!*' she gasped. 'Oh!'

Cecily saw Algernon coming towards them from the house. 'Here,' she said, 'is my Ernest.'

Seeming not to notice the others, Algernon went straight over to her. 'My own love!' he said, and bent to kiss her.

Cecily drew back. 'One moment, Ernest,' she said sternly. 'May I ask you, are you engaged to be married to this young lady?'

'To what young lady?' Algernon asked. He looked round and then gasped, 'Good heavens! Gwendolen!'

'Yes,' said Cecily. 'To Good heavens Gwendolen— I mean, to Gwendolen.'

Algernon laughed. 'Of course not! What could have put such an idea into your pretty little head?'

'Thank you,' said Cecily, presenting her cheek to him. 'You may kiss me.' He promptly did so.

Gwendolen smiled graciously. 'I felt there was some slight error, Miss Cardew,' she observed. 'The gentleman who is now embracing you is my cousin, Mr. Algernon Moncrieff.'

Breaking away from him in distaste, Cecily exclaimed, 'Algernon Moncrieff! *Algernon*? Oh!'

The two young ladies moved towards each other, putting their arms around each other's waists as if for protection. They faced the men angrily.

'Are you called Algernon?' Cecily asked her suitor sharply.

Looking extremely chastened, Algernon replied, 'I cannot deny it.'

'Oh!' It seemed as though Cecily was about to faint.

Gwendolen addressed Jack. 'Is your name really *John?*' she asked, uttering the name in a tone of the utmost distaste.

Jack stood proudly. 'I could deny it if I liked,' he answered. 'I could deny anything if I liked. But my name certainly is John. It has been John for years.'

Cecily looked at Gwendolen. 'A gross deception has been practised on both of us,' she said.

'My poor wounded Cecily!' Gwendolen cooed.

'My sweet wronged Gwendolen!' Cecily responded.

Slowly and seriously, Gwendolen asked Cecily, 'You will call me "sister", will you not?' They embraced, while Jack and Algernon walked up and down, groaning.

'There is just one question I would like to be allowed to ask my guardian,' Cecily told Gwendolen in an urgent tone.

'An admirable idea!' Gwendolen responded, apparently reading her friend's mind. Deciding to speak for them both, she turned to Jack. 'Mr. Worthing,' she said, 'there is just one question I would like to be permitted to put to you. Where is your brother Ernest? We are both engaged to be married to your brother Ernest, so it is a matter of some importance to us to know where your brother Ernest is at present.'

Jack Worthing stepped forward. 'Gwendolen . . . Cecily . . .' he said, slowly and hesitatingly, 'it is very painful for me to be forced to speak the truth. It is the first time in my life that I have ever been reduced to such a painful position, and I am really quite inexperienced in doing anything of the kind.' He paused, cast a baleful glance at Algernon, and continued, 'However, I will tell you quite frankly that I have no brother Ernest. I have no brother at all. I never had a brother in my life, and I certainly have not the smallest intention of ever having one in the future.'

Cecily looked extremely surprised to hear this. 'No brother at all?' she queried.

'None,' Jack replied, cheerfully.

In a decidedly severe tone, Gwendolen asked, 'Have you never had a brother of any kind?'

'Never,' Jack answered her pleasantly. 'Not even of any kind.'

The two young women looked at each other, and then Gwendolen said, 'I am afraid it is quite clear, Cecily, that neither of us is engaged to be married to anyone.'

Cecily nodded in agreement. 'It is not a very pleasant position for a young girl suddenly to find herself in, is it?'

'Let us go into the house,' said Gwendolen. 'They will hardly venture to come after us there.'

'No, men are so cowardly, aren't they?' Cecily agreed. They linked arms and retired towards the house, casting scornful looks at the men as they left.

Jack Worthing and Algernon Moncrieff glumly watched them go. Then Jack rounded furiously on his friend. 'This ghastly state of things is what you call Bunburying, I suppose?' he snarled.

'Yes,' Algernon replied, complacently. 'And a perfectly wonderful Bunbury it is. The most wonderful Bunbury I have ever had in my life.'

'Well, you've no right whatsoever to Bunbury here,' was the exasperated retort.

'That is absurd,' Algernon told him. 'One has a right to Bunbury anywhere one chooses. Every serious Bunburyist knows that.'

'Serious Bunburyist?' Jack snorted in disgust. 'Good heavens!'

'After all,' Algernon explained patiently, 'one must be serious about something, if one wants to have any amusement in life. I happen to be serious about Bunburying.' He regarded his friend with an air of affection mixed with solicitude. 'What on earth you are serious about I haven't got the remotest idea. About everything, I should fancy. You have such an absolutely trivial nature.'

Suppressing a desire to throttle Algernon, Jack exclaimed testily, 'Well, the only small satisfaction I have in the whole of this wretched business is that your friend Bunbury is quite exploded. You won't be able to run down to the country quite so often as you used to do, dear Algy. And a very good thing too.'

The look on Algernon's face could only be described as a smirk. 'Your brother is a little off-colour, isn't he, dear Jack?' he pointed out maliciously. 'You won't be able to disappear to London quite so frequently as your wicked custom was. And not a bad thing either.'

Ignoring this, Jack continued, 'As for your conduct towards Miss Cardew, I must say that your taking in a sweet, simple, innocent girl like that is quite inexcusable. To say nothing of the fact that she is my ward.'

'I can see no possible defence at all,' Algernon retorted coolly, 'for your deceiving a brilliant, clever, thoroughly experienced young lady like Miss Fairfax. To say nothing of the fact that she is my cousin.'

'I wanted to be engaged to Gwendolen, that is all,' Jack said defensively, adding, 'I love her.'

'Well,' his friend replied, 'I simply wanted to be engaged to Cecily. I adore her.'

Jack snorted again, this time in derision. 'There is certainly no chance of your marrying Miss Cardew,' he assured Algernon.

Algernon assumed a gravely reflective expression. 'I don't think there is much likelihood, Jack,' he advised, 'of you and Miss Fairfax being united.'

'Well, that is no business of yours,' Jack snapped.

Algernon raised an eyebrow. 'If it was my business, I wouldn't talk about it,' he stated calmly. Picking up a muffin from the dish on the table, he began to eat. 'It is very vulgar to talk about one's business. Only people like stockbrokers do that, and then merely at dinner parties.'

'How you can sit there,' Jack expostulated, 'calmly eating muffins when we are in this horrible trouble, I can't make out.' With as stern a tone as he could summon up, he added, 'You seem to me to be perfectly heartless.'

'Well, I can't eat muffins in an agitated manner,' said Algernon reasonably. 'The butter would probably get on my cuffs.' He took another. 'One should always eat muffins quite calmly. It is the only way to eat them.'

Jack continued to glare at him. 'I say it's perfectly heartless your eating muffins at all, under the circumstances,' he insisted.

Algernon remained unmoved. 'When I am in trouble,' he said nonchalantly, 'eating is the only thing that consoles me. Indeed, when I am in really great trouble, as someone who knows me as intimately as you ought to know already, I refuse everything except food and drink.' Rising from the table with the plate of muffins in his hand, he concluded, 'Besides, I am particularly fond of muffins.'

'Nevertheless, there is no reason why you should eat them all in that greedy way,' said Jack. He took the plate of muffins away and selected one for himself.

Algernon snatched up from the table a plate containing tea-cake and offered it to Jack, attempting to exchange it for the muffins. 'I wish you would have tea-cake instead,' he said. 'I don't like tea-cake.'

'Good heavens!' exclaimed Jack, by now completely exasperated. 'I suppose a man may eat his own muffins in his own garden.'

'But you have just said it was perfectly heartless to eat muffins,' Algernon pointed out.

'I said it was perfectly heartless of you, under the circumstances,' his friend explained. 'That is a very different thing.'

'That may be,' Algernon replied. 'But the muffins are the same.' He seized the plate from Jack and stuffed another muffin in his mouth.

Jack looked at him despondently. 'Algy,' he sighed, 'I wish to goodness you would go.'

Algernon looked shocked. 'You can't possibly ask me to go without having some dinner,' he said. 'It's absurd. I never go without my dinner. No one ever does, except vegetarians and people like that.' He thought for a moment, and then, remembering, added, 'Besides, I have just made arrangements with Dr. Chasuble to be christened at a quarter to six under the name of Ernest.'

'My dear fellow,' said Jack loftily, 'the sooner you give up that nonsense the better. I myself made arrangements this morning with Dr. Chasuble to be christened at five-thirty, and I naturally will take the name of Ernest. Gwendolen would wish it.'

When Algernon made no reply, Jack continued, irritably, 'We can't both be christened Ernest. It's absurd. Besides,' he added, more calmly, 'I have a perfect right to be christened if I like. There is no evidence at all that I have ever been christened by anybody. I should think it extremely probable I never was, and so does Dr. Chasuble. It is entirely different in your case. You have been christened already.'

'Yes,' Algernon confessed reluctantly, 'but I have not been christened for years.'

'Yes, but you have been christened,' Jack insisted. 'That is the important thing.'

'Quite so,' Algernon agreed. 'So I know my consti-
tution can stand it.' He gave his friend a look of
compassion. 'If you are not quite sure about your
ever having been christened, I must say I think it
rather dangerous your venturing on it now. It might
make you very unwell. You can hardly have forgotten,'
he continued pointedly, 'that someone very closely
connected with you was very nearly carried off this
week in Paris by a severe chill.'

Jack considered this for a moment, then replied, 'Yes,
but you said yourself that a severe chill was not
hereditary.'

'It usen't to be, I know,' Algernon admitted. 'But I
daresay it is now. Science is always making wonderful
improvements in things.'

'Oh, that is nonsense,' said Jack, picking up the
muffin-plate from the table, where Algernon had
incautiously laid it down. 'You are always talking
nonsense.'

'Jack, you are eating the muffins again!' Algernon
exclaimed. 'I wish you wouldn't. There are only two
left.' He snatched them up. 'I told you I was particularly fond of muffins.'

'But I hate tea-cake,' cried Jack.

'Why on earth, then,' his friend asked reasonably,
'do you allow tea-cake to be served up for your guests?
What ideas you have of hospitality!'

Jack's temper flared up. 'Algernon!' he shouted. 'I
have already told you to go. I don't want you here.
Why don't you go?'

Algernon contemplated him calmly. 'I haven't quite

finished my tea yet,' he said. 'And I see there is still one muffin left.'

Jack groaned, sank into a chair, and buried his face in his hands. Algernon serenely continued eating.

CHAPTER
ELEVEN

CHAPTER ELEVEN

G WENDOLEN and Cecily stood at the french windows in the drawing-room, looking out at the two men.

'The fact that they did not follow us at once into the house, as anyone else would have done,' Gwendolen observed, 'seems to me to show that they have some sense of shame left.'

Cecily rubbed a window-pane unnecessarily. 'They have been eating muffins,' she said. 'That looks like repentance.'

Gwendolen seemed unconvinced. She paused awhile, and then said, 'They don't seem to notice us at all. Couldn't you cough?'

'But I haven't got a cough,' Cecily replied.

'Oh, they're looking at us,' Gwendolen exclaimed suddenly. 'What effrontery!'

'They're approaching,' Cecily remarked. 'That's very forward of them.'

Gwendolen regarded her friend gravely. 'Let us preserve a dignified silence,' she suggested.

'Certainly,' Cecily agreed. 'It's the only thing to do now.'

They turned to face the door as it opened and Jack entered, followed by Algernon, both whistling a popular tune from a Gilbert and Sullivan opera.

The young women looked at each other in dismay. 'Our dignified silence seems to have produced a most unpleasant effect,' said Gwendolen.

'An extremely distasteful one,' Cecily agreed.

'But we will not be the first to speak,' Gwendolen cautioned.

'Certainly not,' said Cecily.

Immediately breaking her own injunction, Gwendolen addressed Jack. 'Mr. Worthing, I have something very particular to ask you. Much depends on your reply.'

Cecily nodded in agreement. 'Gwendolen, your common sense is invaluable.' She turned to Algernon. 'Mr. Moncrieff,' she asked with cold formality, 'would you kindly answer me the following question. Why did you pretend to be my guardian's brother?'

'In order, my dear Miss Cecily, that I might have an opportunity of meeting you,' was Algernon's immediate and glibly delivered reply.

Cecily looked at Gwendolen. 'That certainly seems a satisfactory explanation, does it not?' she asked.

'Yes, dear, if you can believe him,' Gwendolen replied with a certain sarcasm in her tone.

'I don't,' said Cecily. 'But that does not affect the wonderful beauty of his answer.'

'True,' Gwendolen conceded. 'In matters of grave importance, it is style, not sincerity, that is the vital thing.' She turned to Jack. 'Mr. Worthing,' she asked, 'what explanation can you offer to me for pretending to have a brother?'

Jack opened his mouth to reply, but before he could speak Gwendolen held up an admonitory hand. 'Was it,' she prompted him hastily and, indeed, helpfully, 'in order that you might have an opportunity of coming up to town to see me as often as possible?'

Jack placed a hand over his heart. 'Can you doubt it, Miss Fairfax?'

'I have the gravest doubts upon the subject, but I intend to crush them. This is not the moment for German scepticism,' she replied. She turned to Cecily and said, 'Their explanations appear to be quite satisfactory. Especially Mr. Worthing's. That seems to me to have the stamp of truth upon it.'

Cecily nodded. 'I am more than content with what Mr. Moncrieff said,' she confided. 'His voice alone inspires one with absolute credulity.'

'Then you think we should forgive them?' asked Gwendolen.

'Yes,' said Cecily with emphasis. 'I mean no,' she added hastily.

'True!' Gwendolen exclaimed. 'I had forgotten. There are principles at stake that one cannot surrender.' She glanced at Cecily in consternation. 'Which of us should tell them?' she wondered. 'The task is not a pleasant one.'

Cecily looked thoughtful. 'Could we not both speak at the same time?' she suggested.

'An excellent idea,' said Gwendolen. 'I nearly always speak at the same time as other people.' She beamed at Cecily. 'Will you take the time from me?' she asked.

'Certainly,' Cecily replied. She watched Gwendolen, who raised her right arm and beat time with an uplifted forefinger.

In unison, the two young ladies announced, 'Your Christian names are still an insuperable barrier. That is all!'

'Our Christian names!' Algernon and Jack echoed, also in unison. 'Is that all? But we are going to be christened this afternoon.'

Gwendolen gave Jack a look of the utmost admiration. 'For my sake you are prepared to do this terrible thing?' she asked.

'I am,' Jack replied proudly.

Cecily addressed Algernon. 'To please me you are ready to face this fearful ordeal?'

'I am,' he assured her.

Gwendolen turned to Cecily. 'How absurd,' she observed, 'to talk of the equality of the sexes. Where questions of self-sacrifice are concerned, men are infinitely beyond us.'

'We are,' Jack agreed, shaking Algernon's hand in comradely fashion.

Cecily concurred with her friend's estimate of the male sex. 'They have moments of physical courage,' she said, 'of which we women know absolutely nothing.'

'Darling!' Gwendolen exclaimed as she fell into Jack's arms.

'Darling!' Algernon echoed as he embraced Cecily.

None of them noticed that Merriman had entered

the drawing-room, followed by a certain formidable personage. Coughing loudly to attract their attention, the butler announced, 'Lady Bracknell.'

'Good heavens!' Jack exclaimed. The two couples separated in alarm, and Merriman left the room as suavely and silently as he had entered it.

Lady Bracknell had fixed her daughter with a stony gaze. 'Gwendolen!' she trumpeted. 'What does this mean?'

'Merely that I am engaged to be married to Mr. Worthing, Mamma,' Gwendolen replied calmly.

'Come here. Sit down,' her mother ordered. When she was not instantly obeyed, she repeated her command more emphatically. 'Sit down immediately, Gwendolen. Hesitation of any kind is a sign of mental decay in the young, and of physical weakness in the old.'

Gwendolen sat down, meekly, and Lady Bracknell turned to Jack. 'Apprised, sir,' she began, 'of my daughter's sudden flight by her trusty maid, whose confidence I purchased by means of a small coin, I followed her at once by a luggage train.' She glared at everyone in the room, perhaps recalling the discomfort of her journey, and blaming them personally for it. Then she continued, 'Her unhappy father is, I am glad to say, under the impression that she is attending a more than usually lengthy lecture by the University Extension Scheme on the Influence of a Permanent Income on Thought. I do not propose to undeceive him.'

She paused, her thoughts dwelling momentarily on

Lord Bracknell. 'Indeed,' she resumed, 'I have never undeceived him on any question. I would consider it wrong. But, of course,' and her gaze was now directed firmly at Jack Worthing, 'you will clearly understand that all communication between yourself and my daughter must cease immediately from this moment. On this point, as indeed on all points, I am firm.'

Jack did not allow himself to be put out of countenance by Lady Bracknell's words. He merely replied, politely, 'I am engaged to be married to Gwendolen, Lady Bracknell.'

Lady Bracknell's rejoinder was swift and to the point. 'You are nothing of the kind, sir,' she informed him. Deciding that the matter was now satisfactorily settled, she turned her attention to her nephew. 'And now, as regards Algernon—' Again she paused, her gaze now directed at her nephew, but Algernon had allowed his attention to stray from Lady Bracknell, and was beaming idiotically at Cecily. 'Algernon!' Lady Bracknell exclaimed in her most carrying tone.

Algernon looked at her amiably. 'Yes, Aunt Augusta?' he replied.

'May I ask,' his aunt demanded, 'if it is in this house that your invalid friend Mr. Bunbury resides?'

Taken by surprise, Algernon stammered, 'Oh! N-no, B-Bunbury d-doesn't l-live here. Er ... B-Bunbury is somewhere else at present.' With sudden inspiration and an equally sudden return of confidence, he added, 'In fact, Bunbury is dead.'

'*Dead*?' Lady Bracknell looked more affronted than

upset. 'When did Mr. Bunbury die?' she asked. 'His death must have been extremely sudden.'

Algernon's sang-froid had now completely returned. 'Oh!' he replied airily, 'I killed Bunbury this afternoon—I mean, poor Bunbury died this afternoon.'

Lady Bracknell was still curious. 'What did he die of?'

'Bunbury? Oh, he was quite exploded.' Algernon seemed to think this was sufficient explanation.

'*Exploded*!' his aunt exclaimed. 'Was he the victim of a revolutionary outrage?' She looked about the room in some confusion. 'I was not aware,' she admitted, 'that Mr. Bunbury was interested in social legislation. If so, he is well punished for his morbidity.'

'My dear Aunt Augusta,' explained Algernon, 'what I mean is that he was found out. That is, the doctors found out that Bunbury could not live. So Bunbury died.' He smiled happily, turned to Cecily and took her hand in his.

'He seems to have had great confidence in the opinion of his physicians,' Lady Bracknell observed. She shook her head. 'I am glad, however, that he made up his mind at the last to some definite course of action, and I suppose it is a good thing that he acted under proper medical advice.' Turning her attention to matters of more immediate importance, she continued, 'And now that we have finally got rid of this Mr. Bunbury, may I ask, Mr. Worthing, who is that young person whose hand my nephew Algernon is holding in what seems to me a peculiarly unnecessary manner?'

'That lady,' Jack answered, 'is Miss Cecily Cardew, my ward.'

Lady Bracknell bowed coldly to Cecily, and Algernon explained, 'I am engaged to be married to Cecily, Aunt Augusta.'

'I beg your pardon?' his aunt exclaimed.

Cecily ventured a shy smile at Lady Bracknell. 'Mr. Moncrieff and I are engaged to be married, Lady Bracknell,' she confirmed.

Lady Bracknell shivered, went across to a sofa, and sat down. 'I do not know,' she remarked coldly, 'whether there is anything peculiarly exciting in the air of this particular part of Hertfordshire, but the number of engagements that go on seems to me considerably above the proper average that statistics have laid down for our guidance. I think some preliminary enquiry on my part would not be out of place. 'Mr. Worthing,' she asked, in a supercilious tone, 'is Miss Cardew at all connected with any of the larger railway stations in London? I merely desire information. Until yesterday, I had no idea that there were any families or persons whose origin was a terminus.'

Jack looked perfectly furious, but restrained himself. In a cold, clear voice, he replied, 'Miss Cardew is the granddaughter of the late Mr. Thomas Cardew of 149 Belgrave Square, S.W.; Gervase Park, Dorking, Surrey; and the Sporran, Fifeshire, North Britain.'

Lady Bracknell looked at first surprised and then reflective. 'That sounds not unsatisfactory,' she observed judicially. 'Three addresses always inspire confidence, even in tradesmen. But,' she asked, 'what proof have I of their authenticity?'

Jack's voice became colder. 'I have carefully preserved the Court Guides of the period,' he said. 'They are open to your inspection, Lady Bracknell.'

'I have known strange errors in that publication,' she retorted grimly.

Affecting not to have heard her, Jack continued, 'Miss Cardew's family solicitors are Messrs. Markby, Markby and Markby.'

'Markby, Markby and Markby?' Lady Bracknell echoed. She sounded almost approving. 'A firm of the very highest position in their profession. Indeed, I am told that one of the Mr. Markbys is occasionally to be seen at dinner parties. So far, I am satisfied.'

Jack made no attempt to keep the extreme irritability out of his voice as he replied, 'How extremely kind of you, Lady Bracknell. I have also in my possession, you will be pleased to hear, certificates of Miss Cardew's birth, baptism, whooping cough, registration, vaccination, confirmation, and the measles—both the German and the English variety.'

'Ah, a life crowded with incident, I see,' her ladyship observed, 'though perhaps somewhat too exciting for a young girl. I am not myself in favour of premature experiences.' She rose and looked at her watch. 'Gwendolen,' she announced, 'the time approaches for our departure. We have not a moment to lose.' She moved to the door, but turned back. 'As a matter of form, Mr. Worthing,' she asked, 'perhaps I had better know if Miss Cardew has any little fortune?'

'Oh,' Jack responded with a tight smile, 'about a hundred and thirty thousand pounds in the Funds. That is all. Goodbye, Lady Bracknell. So pleased to have seen you.'

CHAPTER
TWELVE

CHAPTER TWELVE

At Jack's announcement of Cecily's financial situation, Lady Bracknell ceased her stately progress towards the door. Turning, she surveyed him intently. 'A moment, Mr. Worthing,' she said, and with that she returned to her seat.

When she had made herself comfortable, she looked at Jack again and exclaimed, 'A hundred and thirty thousand pounds! And in the Funds!' She turned her gaze upon Cecily. 'Miss Cardew,' she observed, 'seems to me a most attractive young lady, now that I look at her properly. Few girls of the present day have any really solid qualities, any of the qualities that last, and improve with time.' Looking around at the others, she complained, 'We live, I regret to say, in an age of surfaces.'

She turned her attention back to Cecily. 'Come over here, dear,' she commanded.

Cecily went across to her. 'Pretty child!' Lady Bracknell murmured. Examining her from top to toe, she went on, 'Your dress is sadly simple, and your hair seems almost as Nature might have left it.' For a moment she was silent, and then she nodded decisively. 'We can soon alter all that, however. A thoroughly experienced French maid produces a really marvellous result in a very brief space of time.' She smiled reminiscently. 'I remember recommending one to young Lady Lancing, and after three months her own husband did not know her.'

'And after six months,' Jack muttered, 'nobody knew her.'

Lady Bracknell glared at him; then, with a practised smile, she addressed Cecily again. 'Kindly turn around, sweet child.'

The girl turned around completely. 'No,' said Lady Bracknell, 'the side view is what I want.'

Cecily obediently presented her profile, and her ladyship observed, 'Yes, quite as I expected. There are distinct social possibilities in your profile. The two weak points in our age are its want of principle and its want of profile.' Then, to Cecily once more: 'The chin a little higher, dear. Style largely depends on the way the chin is worn. They are worn very high just at present.'

When she was satisfied by the angle at which Cecily was attempting to wear her chin, Lady Bracknell turned to her nephew, who had been observing the proceedings with a rather anxious smile on his face, and summoned him with a peremptory 'Algernon!'

'Yes, Aunt Augusta.'

'There are distinct social possibilities in Miss Cardew's profile,' she assured him.

'Cecily,' Algernon replied, 'is the sweetest, dearest, prettiest girl in the whole world. And I don't care twopence about social possibilities.'

His aunt looked disapproving. 'Never speak disrespectfully of society, Algernon,' she said. 'Only people who can't get into it do that.'

She turned back to Cecily. 'Dear child,' she continued, 'of course you know that Algernon has nothing but his debts to depend upon. But I do not approve of mercenary marriages. When I married Lord Bracknell, I had no fortune of any kind. But I never dreamed for a moment of allowing that to stand in my way.'

She paused, surveyed the assembled company again, and then said graciously, 'Well, I suppose I must give my consent.'

'Thank you, Aunt Augusta,' Algernon breathed rapturously.

'Cecily, you may kiss me,' said Lady Bracknell. The invitation bore a distinct note of command.

'Thank you, Lady Bracknell,' Cecily murmured, and she complied.

'You may also address me as Aunt Augusta for the future,' she was told, at which she promptly amended her reply to 'Thank you, Aunt Augusta.'

Lady Bracknell looked quite satisfied. 'The marriage, I think, had better take place quite soon,' she observed. This, too, sounded like an instruction.

'Thank you, Aunt Augusta,' Algernon and Cecily murmured, almost in unison.

'To be absolutely frank,' Lady Bracknell continued, 'I am not in favour of long engagements. They give people the opportunity of finding out each other's character before marriage, which I think is never advisable.'

She would have said more, but Jack Worthing inter-vened. 'I beg your pardon for interrupting you, Lady Bracknell,' he said smoothly, 'but this engagement is quite out of the question. I am Miss Cardew's guardian, and she cannot marry without my consent until she comes of age.' He paused for effect, and then added, 'That consent I absolutely decline to give.'

'Upon what grounds, may I ask?' Lady Bracknell demanded indignantly. She gestured towards her nephew. 'Algernon is an extremely, I may almost say an ostentatiously, eligible young man. He has nothing, but he looks everything. What more can one desire?'

Jack rubbed his hands together, unclasped them, and looked down at them as though for inspiration. Then, choosing his words with great care, he began to speak. 'It pains me very much to have to speak frankly to you, Lady Bracknell, about your nephew, but the fact is that I do not approve at all of his moral character. I suspect him of being untruthful.'

Algernon and Cecily looked at him in indignant amazement, while Algernon's aunt exclaimed, 'Untruthful? My nephew Algernon? Impossible! He was educated at Oxford.'

'I fear there can be no possible doubt about the matter,' Jack replied. 'This afternoon, during my temporary absence in London on an important ques-tion of romance, he obtained admission to this house by means of the false pretence of being my brother.' Warming to his subject, he continued, 'What is more, under an assumed name he drank, I have just been informed by my butler, an entire pint bottle of my

Perrier-Jouet, Brut, '89—a wine I was specially reserving for myself. Continuing his disgraceful deception, he succeeded in the course of the afternoon in alienating the affections of my only ward. He subsequently stayed to tea, and devoured every single muffin.' Jack glared at Algernon. 'And what makes his conduct all the more heartless, is that he was perfectly well aware from the first that I have no brother, that I never had a brother, and that I don't intend to have a brother, not even of any kind. I distinctly told him so myself yesterday afternoon.'

Lady Bracknell had listened impassively to Jack's tirade. When he finished, she coughed to gain her audience's attention, then announced regally, 'Mr. Worthing, after careful consideration I have decided entirely to overlook my nephew's conduct to you.'

Jack gave a tight smile. 'That is very generous of you, Lady Bracknell. My own decision, however, is unalterable. I decline to give my consent.'

Lady Bracknell glared at him, and then turned to Cecily. 'Come here, sweet child,' she said. Cecily approached, and Lady Bracknell asked, with an attempt at tenderness, 'How old are you, dear?'

'Well,' Cecily replied, 'I am really only eighteen, but I always admit to twenty when I go to evening parties.'

'You are perfectly right in making some slight alteration,' Lady Bracknell assured her. 'Indeed, no woman should ever be quite accurate about her age. It looks so calculating.' In a meditative manner, she whispered to herself, 'Eighteen, but admitting to twenty at evening parties.' Then she continued, firmly, 'Well, it will not be very long before you are of age, and free from the restraints of tutelage. So I don't think that your guardian's consent is, after all, a matter of any importance.'

Jack, his expression bordering on the smug, intervened once more. 'Pray excuse me, Lady Bracknell, for interrupting you again,' he said, 'but it is only fair to tell you that, according to the terms of her grandfather's will, Miss Cardew does not come legally of age until she is thirty-five.'

Lady Bracknell looked at him blandly. 'That does not seem to me to be a grave objection,' she asserted. 'London society is full of women of the very highest birth who have, of their own free choice, remained thirty-five for years.' Emitting a sound just distinguishable as a laugh, she continued, 'Lady Dumbleton is an instance in point. To my own knowledge she has been thirty-five ever since she arrived at the age of forty, which was many years ago now.'

She surveyed her audience complacently. 'No,' she declared, 'I see no reason why our dear Cecily should not be even still more attractive at the age you mention than she is at present. And,' she added pensively, 'there will be a large accumulation of property.'

'Algy,' Cecily asked, her voice quivering with emotion, 'could you wait for me till I was thirty-five?'

'Of course I could, Cecily,' he replied without a moment's hesitation. 'You know I could.'

'Yes, I felt it instinctively,' said Cecily. Her voice, however, betrayed her apprehension. 'But *I* couldn't wait all that time. I hate waiting even five minutes for anybody. It always makes me rather cross. I am not punctual myself, I know, but I do like punctuality in others, and waiting, even to be married, is quite out of the question.'

Algernon looked at her in dismay. 'Then what is to be done, Cecily?' he asked despairingly.

'I don't know, Mr. Moncrieff,' she replied primly.

Somewhat testily, Lady Bracknell said, 'My dear Mr. Worthing, as Miss Cardew states positively that she cannot wait till she is thirty-five—a remark which I am bound to say seems to me to show a somewhat impatient nature—I would beg of you to reconsider your decision. I am certain that—'

Jack interrupted unceremoniously. 'My dear Lady Bracknell,' he declared, 'the matter is entirely in your own hands. The moment you consent to my marriage with your daughter Gwendolen, I will most gladly allow your nephew to form an alliance with my ward.'

Lady Bracknell rose and, drawing herself up to her full height, said firmly, 'You must be quite aware that what you propose is out of the question.'

'In that case,' replied Jack with equal firmness, 'a passionate celibacy is all that any of us can look forward to.'

'That is not the destiny I propose for Gwendolen,' Lady Bracknell announced. 'Algernon, of course, can choose for himself.' She pulled out her watch and consulted it. 'Come, dear,' she ordered Gwendolen. 'We have already missed five, if not six, trains. To miss any more might expose us to comment on the platform.'

Gwendolen rose and moved obediently to her mother's side.

CHAPTER
THIRTEEN

CHAPTER THIRTEEN

AS Lady Bracknell was beginning her stately progress from the room, followed meekly by Gwendolen, the door suddenly opened and Dr. Chasuble entered. Beaming at Algernon and Jack, he said, 'I am delighted to tell you that everything is quite ready for the christenings.'

Lady Bracknell turned abruptly to face him. 'The christenings, sir?' she exclaimed, her visage as wrathful as her voice. 'Is not that somewhat premature?'

Dr. Chasuble looked puzzled. Pointing to Jack and Algernon, he explained, 'Both these gentlemen have expressed a desire for immediate baptism.'

'At their age?' Lady Bracknell gasped. 'The idea is grotesque and irreligious!' She turned to her nephew. 'Algernon, I forbid you to be baptized,' she ordered. 'I will not hear of such excesses. Lord Bracknell would be highly displeased if he learned that this was the way in which you wasted your time and money.'

Looking about him in consternation, Dr. Chasuble asked plaintively, 'Am I to understand then that there are to be no christenings at all this afternoon?'

149

Jack felt obliged to intervene. 'I don't think, Dr. Chasuble,' he said, 'that, as things are now, it would be of much practical value to either of us.'

Much affronted, the Rector said, 'I am grieved to hear such sentiments from you, Mr. Worthing. They savour of the heretical views of the Anabaptists, views that I have completely refuted in four of my unpublished sermons.'

He eyed the assembly sternly, then turned once more to Jack. 'However, as your present mood seems to be one peculiarly secular, I will return to the church at once. Indeed, I have just been informed by the pew-opener that for the last hour and a half Miss Prism has been waiting for me in the vestry.'

He turned to go, only to be halted by a startled exclamation from Lady Bracknell. '*Prism*? Miss Prism?' Beckoning him closer, she stared intently into his face. 'Did I hear you mention a Miss Prism?' she asked, greatly agitated.

'Yes, Lady Bracknell,' Dr. Chasuble replied, wonderingly. 'I am on my way to join her.'

'Pray allow me to detain you for a moment,' Lady Bracknell commanded, as she attempted to regain her composure. 'This matter may prove to be one of vital importance to Lord Bracknell and myself.' She took a deep breath, and then asked, 'Is this Miss Prism a female of repellent aspect, remotely connected with education?'

Somewhat indignantly, Canon Chasuble replied, 'She is the most cultivated of ladies, and the very picture of respectability.'

'It is obviously the same person,' Lady Bracknell observed with satisfaction. 'May I ask what position she holds in your household?'

'Madam,' Dr. Chasuble informed her severely, 'I am a celibate.'

'Miss Prism,' Jack explained to Lady Bracknell, 'has been for the last three years Miss Cardew's esteemed governess and valued companion.'

Lady Bracknell was clearly still in distress. 'In spite of what I hear of her,' she exclaimed, 'I must see her at once. Let her be sent for.'

Jack was considering how best to accomplish this when Dr. Chasuble, who had chanced to glance out of the window, remarked, 'She approaches. She is nigh.'

Everyone looked out of the window. Miss Prism could indeed be seen coming across the lawn. A suspenseful silence reigned for some moments until the governess hurriedly entered the room.

Addressing Dr. Chasuble, Miss Prism said in a tone of slight reproach, 'I was told you expected me in the vestry, dear Canon. I have been waiting for you there for an hour and three-quarters.'

Glancing around, she caught sight of Lady Bracknell, who had fixed her with her stony glare. Miss Prism grew pale. She quailed, and looked anxiously around as if desirous of escape.

'*Prism*!' Lady Bracknell thundered. The governess bowed her head as though in shame. In a severe, judicial voice, Lady Bracknell ordered, 'Come here, Prism!' Miss Prism now approached her in a humble manner.

'Prism!' her ladyship asked in sternly measured tones, 'Where is that baby?'

General consternation ensued. The Canon started back in horror, while Algernon and Jack, looking anxious, embraced Cecily and Gwendolen as though to protect them from hearing the details of what might prove to be a terrible public scandal.

'Twenty-eight years ago, Prism,' Lady Bracknell said, fixing the governess with an accusing eye, 'you left Lord Bracknell's house, Number 104, Upper Grosvenor Square, in charge of a perambulator that contained a baby of the male sex. You never returned. A few weeks later, through the elaborate investigations of the Metropolitan Police, the perambulator was discovered at midnight standing by itself in a remote corner of Hyde Park. It contained the manuscript of a three-volume novel of more than usually revolting sentimentality.'

Miss Prism gave a start of involuntary indignation at hearing her lost novel thus described. Ignoring this reaction, Lady Bracknell continued, 'But the baby was not there.'

Everyone looked at Miss Prism in horrified fascination.

'Prism,' Lady Bracknell asked once again, 'where is that baby?'

Silence reigned. Then, quaveringly, Miss Prism began to speak. 'Lady Bracknell, I admit with shame that I do not know. I only wish I did. The plain facts of the case are these. On the morning of the day you mention, a day that is for ever branded on my memory, I prepared as usual to take the baby out in its perambulator. I had also with me a somewhat old, but capacious, hand-bag in which I had intended to place the manuscript of a work of fiction that I had written during my few unoccupied hours.'

She looked desperately around the room, then continued, 'In a moment of mental abstraction, for which I can never forgive myself, I deposited the manuscript in the bassinette and placed the baby in the hand-bag.'

Jack had been listening with the closest attention. 'But where did you deposit the hand-bag?' he asked.

Miss Prism looked as though she were about to weep. 'Do not ask me, Mr. Worthing,' she gasped.

'Miss Prism,' Jack urged, 'this is a matter of no small importance to me. I insist on knowing where you deposited the hand-bag that contained that infant.'

The governess shook her head as though trying to rid herself of the memory. 'I left it in the cloakroom of one of the larger railway stations in London,' she said despondently.

'What railway station?' Jack asked, urgently

'Victoria,' replied Miss Prism, sounding quite crushed. 'The Brighton line.' Looking around, she espied a chair, and collapsed into it.

'I must retire to my room for a moment,' Jack announced. 'Gwendolen, wait here for me.'

'If you are not too long, I will wait here for you all my life,' Gwendolen assured him, as Jack left the room in great excitement.

Dr. Chasuble was bewildered. 'What do you think this means, Lady Bracknell?' he asked.

'I dare not even suspect, Dr. Chasuble,' she replied,

her tone regaining its customary hauteur. 'I need hardly tell you that, in families of high position, strange coincidences are not supposed to occur. They are hardly considered the thing.'

Everyone looked up as loud noises suddenly broke out overhead, clearly coming from a room on the floor above. It sounded as if someone was throwing heavy objects about.

'Uncle Jack seems strangely agitated,' Cecily observed anxiously.

'Your guardian has a very emotional nature,' replied the Canon, perhaps hoping to reassure her.

'This noise is extremely unpleasant,' Lady Bracknell complained. 'It sounds as if he was having an argument. I dislike arguments of any kind. They are always vulgar, and often convincing.'

'I think it has stopped now,' said Dr. Chasuble, whereupon the noises began again, redoubled in volume.

'I wish he would arrive at some conclusion,' Lady Bracknell remarked, irritably.

'This suspense is terrible,' Gwendolen said. 'I hope it will last.'

The noise subsided, to be succeeded by the sound of Jack Worthing running down the stairs. He dashed into the room, carrying a large black leather hand-bag. Rushing over to Miss Prism, he thrust it at her.

'Is this the hand-bag, Miss Prism?' he asked. 'Examine it carefully before you speak. The happiness of more than one life depends on your answer.'

Miss Prism examined the hand-bag carefully, as instructed. Then, in a remarkably calm voice, she announced, 'It seems to be mine. Yes, here is the injury it received through the upsetting of a Gower Street omnibus in younger and happier days. Here is the stain on the lining caused by the explosion of a temperance beverage.' She looked up at him and explained, 'That was an incident that occurred at Leamington. And here,' she continued, 'on the lock, are my initials. I had forgotten that in an extravagant mood I had had them placed there. Yes, the bag is undoubtedly mine. I am delighted to have it so unexpectedly restored to me. It has been a great inconvenience being without it all these years.'

'Miss Prism,' said Jack, in a voice choked with emotion, 'more is restored to you than this hand-bag.' She gave him an enquiring look, at which he declared, 'I was the baby you placed in it.'

'You?' Miss Prism gasped in amazement.

'Yes—Mother!' Jack cried, and he embraced her.

Miss Prism recoiled in indignant astonishment. 'Mr. Worthing,' she cried, 'I am unmarried!'

Disconcerted, Jack exclaimed, 'Unmarried! I do not deny that is a serious blow.' He looked at the others, then continued defiantly, 'But, after all, who has the right to cast a stone against one who has suffered? Cannot repentance wipe out an act of folly?' Warming to his theme, he went on, 'Why should there be one law for men, and another for women?' Again attempting to embrace her, he proclaimed, 'Mother, I forgive you.'

Miss Prism leapt up from her chair. 'Mr. Worthing, there is some error,' she said indignantly. Pointing to

Lady Bracknell, she declared, 'There is the lady who can tell you who you really are.'

In the silence that followed, Jack looked steadily at her ladyship, paused for a moment, and then asked with studied courtesy, 'Lady Bracknell, I hate to seem inquisitive, but would you kindly inform me who I am?'

Lady Bracknell surveyed him, not without interest. Then, 'I am afraid that the news I have to give you will not altogether please you,' she answered. 'You are the son of my poor sister, Mrs. Moncrieff, and consequently Algernon's elder brother.'

Whatever effect she felt her words might have had upon Jack, she could not have envisaged his reaction. 'Algy's elder brother!' he shouted delightedly. 'Then I have a brother after all. I knew I had a brother! I always said I had a brother!' He turned to Cecily. 'Cecily—how could you have ever doubted that I had a brother?' Seizing Algernon, he began to introduce him to everyone. 'Dr. Chasuble, meet my unfortunate brother. Miss Prism, my unfortunate brother. Gwendolen, my unfortunate brother.' He embraced Algernon and then, holding him at arm's length, said reprovingly, 'Algy, you young scoundrel, you will have to treat me with more respect in the future. You have never behaved to me like a brother in all your life.'

'Well, not till today, old boy, I admit,' Algernon replied. 'I did my best this afternoon, however, even though I was out of practice.' The two brothers shook hands warmly.

Gwendolen embraced Jack. 'My own!' she exclaimed. Yet almost at once she drew back. 'But what own are you? What is your Christian name, now that you have become someone else?'

'Good heavens!' cried Jack, 'I had quite forgotten that point.' He looked at her somewhat apprehensively. 'Your decision on the subject of my name is irrevocable, I suppose?'

'Of course,' Gwendolen replied. 'I never change, except in my affections.'

'What a noble nature you have, Gwendolen,' said Cecily, deeply moved.

'Then the question of my name had better be cleared up at once,' said Jack determinedly. 'Aunt Augusta, can you tell me? At the time when Miss Prism left me in the hand-bag, had I been christened already?'

Lady Bracknell looked affronted, although she answered calmly enough. 'Every luxury that money could buy, including christening, had been lavished on you by your fond and doting parents,' she assured him.

'So I was christened,' Jack said. 'That is settled. Now, what name was I given? Let me know the worst.'

'Being the eldest son,' Lady Bracknell informed him, 'you were naturally christened after your father.'

'Yes,' said Jack, irritably, 'but what was my father's Christian name?'

Lady Bracknell thought for a few moments. 'I cannot at the present moment recall what the General's Christian name was,' she admitted. 'But I have no doubt he had one. He was eccentric, I admit, but only in later years. And even that was as a result of the Indian climate, and marriage, and indigestion, and other things of that kind.'

With a groan of exasperation, Jack turned to his newly found brother. 'Algy,' he begged, 'can't you recollect what our father's Christian name was?'

'My dear boy,' said Algy, 'we were never even on speaking terms. He died before I was a year old.'

Jack thought for a moment, and then asked Lady Bracknell, 'His name would appear in the Army Lists of the period, I suppose, Aunt Augusta?'

'The General was essentially a man of peace, except in his domestic life,' she replied. 'But I have no doubt his name would appear in any military directory.'

'Yes, of course. The Army Lists of the last forty years are here.' Jack rushed to the bookcase and began to pull books out of it. 'These delightful records should have been my constant study. Now here's letter M. Generals. Mallam, Maxbohm, Magley—what ghastly names they have—Markby, Migsby, Mobbs, Moncrieff! Lieutenant 1840, Captain, Lieutenant-Colonel, Colonel, General 1869, Christian names, Ernest John.'

Jack put the book down quietly, and said, quite calmly, 'I always told you, Gwendolen, that my name was Ernest, didn't I? Well, it is Ernest after all. I mean, it naturally is Ernest.'

'Yes,' Lady Bracknell affirmed. 'I remember now that the General was called Ernest. I knew I had some particular reason for disliking the name.'

'*Ernest*!' Gwendolen exclaimed. 'My own Ernest! I felt from the first that you could have no other name!'

'Gwendolen,' Jack replied, 'it is a terrible thing for a man to find out suddenly that all his life he has been speaking nothing but the truth. Can you forgive me?'

'I can,' she assured him. 'For I feel that you are certain to change.'

'My own one!' cried Jack, embracing her.

Caught up in the spirit of romance which seemed to be infecting the young people, Canon Chasuble turned hastily to Miss Prism and embraced her with a cry of 'Lætitia!'

'Frederick! At last!' she responded enthusiastically.

'Cecily! At last!' cried Algernon.

'Well, although you are no Ernest, at least you are closely related to an Ernest,' replied Cecily, with only a slight reluctance in her voice. 'And I am entitled to claim a woman's prerogative, am I not. So, very well. Algernon! At last!'

'Gwendolen! At last!' shouted Jack.

'Ernest! At last!' she echoed less noisily.

Lady Bracknell looked on disapprovingly. 'My nephew,' she said to Jack, 'you seem to be displaying signs of triviality.'

'On the contrary, Aunt Augusta,' Jack replied, 'I've now realized for the first time in my life the vital Importance of Being Earnest.'